DER

Please return / renew by date shown.
You can renew it at:
norlink.norfolk.gov.uk
or by telephone: 0344 800 8006
Please have your library card & PIN ready

NORFOLK LIBRARY
AND INFORMATION SERVICE

Kelvin I Jones has written extensively about Sherlock Holmes and his creator, Conan Doyle. He is also the author of many ghost and horror stories and recently published a supernatural children's novel, 'Odin's Eye'.

This is the second in the series of crime novels, featuring his detective, John Bottrell. Kelvin is a creative writing tutor for the University of East Anglia, specialising in crime and horror fiction. He lives with his wife Debbie in Norfolk.

Also by the same Author:

STONE DEAD (The first John Bottrell novel)

ODIN'S EYE
(Nightingale Books)
ISBN: 978 1903491 52 2

Flowers Of Evil

Kelvin I Jones

Flowers Of Evil

Vanguard Press

VANGUARD PAPERBACK

© Copyright 2008
Kelvin I Jones

A CIP catalogue record for this title is
available from the British Library.

ISBN 978 184386 413 4

*Vanguard Press is an imprint of
Pegasus Elliot MacKenzie Publishers Ltd.*
www.pegasuspublishers.com

First Published in 2008

**Vanguard Press
Sheraton House Castle Park
Cambridge England**

Printed & Bound in Great Britain

GIFT

Dedication

To Debbie, My inspiration,
who helped shape the past into the present.

PROLOGUE

The young woman had been standing outside the cinema for at least twenty minutes before she finally decided to go in. She had arrived shortly after 6.30pm and had spent part of the time staring up at the art deco turret of the ABC cinema with its pierced panels and stone spread eagle wings. She was dressed in a plain, black skirt, a grubby brown coat and a cheap white T-shirt. Her hair was also plain, cut to the shoulders in a severe Mary Quant style and her plump young face, peppered with acne, was distorted by harsh black eyeliner, so inexpertly applied.

For some while she paced up and down agitatedly on the opposite side of Whiteladies Road, swinging her white plastic handbag nervously, watching the crowd as they filtered in to the cinema. It was the usual mixture for a Friday evening: a handful of impoverished looking students from Bristol University, a few young, well-heeled nouveau riche types from Clifton, one or two hippies and a smattering of aged pensioners.

She watched each one climb the steps and enter the foyer as the traffic rumbled past her in the direction of the Downs. She seemed ill at ease and at one stage appeared to be holding a long, anguished conversation with herself.

At one point a group of youths emerged from the public house just down from the cinema. One of them sent a loud wolf whistle in her direction, but she did not seem to acknowledge or even hear the raucous challenge. Her dark eyes were fixed on one of the later arrivals: a tall, elegantly dressed woman. She wore a long, white, belted mac with a black beret. Her hair was sleek and well cut, accentuating her smooth, pallid skin and high cheek bones and her striking appearance had already attracted the attention of several men as she made her way down towards the cinema. Climbing the steps she stopped and brought out a packet of Gauloise cigarettes and lit one. For a moment she glanced across at the girl on the other side of the road as if she might have recognised her, then threw the cigarette into the road and entered the foyer.

As soon as she had disappeared from view, the girl crossed the road, looking from left to right. Before she entered the foyer, she glanced up at the hoarding which bore the legend 'Yeux sans visage: X cert'. A grainy, black and white poster showed a young woman peering up at a bespectacled, bearded man who hovered over her, his left hand holding a surgeon's scalpel.

She hurried inside, afraid she would lose sight of her. The woman had the poise and elegance of a dancer. As she collected her ticket, the girl was sure she heard a French accent. She slipped into the dark auditorium, keeping close behind her, following the flickering torchlight to the balcony where, squeezing herself in between two courting couples, she sat down. The woman was directly in front of her now.

The commercials began but the girl was oblivious to them. The palms of her hands were damp with perspiration. The woman had removed her beret and her dark hair glistened in the light. She was wearing a subtle perfume, Christian Dior maybe. The girl resisted the temptation to reach forward and touch the thin silk blouse. She was envious of her beauty and style.

It wasn't long before that familiar panic began to set in. She hated confined spaces and the feelings of claustrophobia almost overcame her. Normally she would avoid crowds and coming to the cinema was a test of her courage and resolve. Strictly speaking she shouldn't be here. She would never normally allow herself to take this risk. But this was different.

Six months ago, she had tracked a woman out to the edge of Leigh Woods. She had lived in one of those large mansions on the edge of dense woodland. She had followed her right up to the driveway and been seen by several passers-by who might have been able to identify her, but by now the urge was too strong. The woman had even turned round at one point and had looked straight at her. She had caught up with her in the end, about fifty yards from the house. She had decided she would do it right there and had already reached into her bag for the knife when the front door opened and a man had appeared in the porch. He'd looked straight past the woman and shouted a challenge. The girl had fled, frustrated.

The film lasted for about an hour and a half. When it finally ended, the French woman stood and beat a brisk retreat towards the exit. She followed immediately, trying to match her pace, determined not to lose her. Outside, the woman found a gap in the traffic and crossed to the other side, with swift athletic steps. When she reached the Clifton Down railway station, she turned right down Imperial Road, then was momentarily lost from sight behind tall beech trees. The girl was breathing fast now, fearful of losing her quarry. Her arms were rigid with tension. She was about fifty yards behind her and the woman had still not noticed she was being followed, yes, she was sure of that.

They were heading for the tall Victorian villas of Redland. Ahead of them was a small area of parkland, adjacent to a church. The girl quickened her pace, she knew now this might be her only chance. As the woman entered the park she came to the entrance of a narrow alleyway. It had to be here, this was the spot. It was perfect. She glanced round, the park was deserted.

She closed on the figure ahead of her and called out. Turning in surprise, the woman smiled and waited for her. The girl asked for the time, her hand gripping the handle of the knife in her pocket. As the woman glanced down at her watch, the girl stepped closer, plunging the knife into the side of the woman's throat. The woman recoiled, staggered, then sank to her knees. The girl scrabbled for the duct tape in her pocket, glancing fearfully around in case she should be discovered. The tearing sound of the tape seemed to echo in the silent park and she wound it tightly round the woman's mouth brutally. The woman's terrified eyes were all she could see. She stabbed her again, once in the chest and then began dragging her by the legs into the alleyway.

The body was heavier than she expected but the adrenaline gave her the strength she needed. She was out of sight now, level with a dilapidated garden gate. She kicked it open, pulling the body through the gap. She was standing in the grounds of a large mansion. It was overgrown, the house being hidden from sight by tall oak trees. On her right stood a squat, brick built structure. She pushed her way through long grass and came level with the entrance. It was an ice house. She had seen one before. The gate was secured by a rusty chain but when she examined it she found the padlock was broken. She wrenched at the chain and within seconds had pulled back the rusty gate.

She stepped into the dark, cool interior, welcoming the safety of the dark, feeling the air on her face. She stood in the silence, her heart slowing, remembering what it had been like as a child when she had been locked in the dark, how she had screamed in fear, beating her fists against the door, calling her mother's name. No one had come. No one had answered her screams. And so in the dark she had learned to love the silence.

She was pulling the legs with all her might. The long grass resisted, snagging at the woman's mac and her underclothes, making her appear like some dishevelled scarecrow. The girl seemed to possess supernatural strength. With a final heave the body slid onto the brick floor. She stood up, brushed the grass from her clothes, then stood staring at the lifeless shape in the gloom. She felt empowered now. She was no longer the ugly, acned child. The child that no one ever noticed, except for a drunken yob shouting from the street. How the roles were reversed.

Stepping closer, she reached into the pocket of the woman's mac and pulled out a small brown wallet, which she slipped into her bag. Then, delivering one last vicious kick, she closed the gate behind her, and walked through the garden and back into the alleyway.

She glanced down at her coat where a series of crimson splashes bore testimony to her grim butchery. It was always the way with the jugular vein. Spotting a builder's skip at the corner of Trelawney Road, she removed the coat and pushed it out of sight between a set of broken chairs and a stained mattress. She looked round but the street was deserted save for a down at heel old man who looked as if he had been at the bottle all day. Smiling, she walked rapidly, past the gates of the Grammar School, her mind still immersed in the cool darkness of the ice house, thinking of its pale resident, newly acquired. She felt an enormous sense of satisfaction and pride.

She glanced up at the darkening sky. It had been a perfect day. Tonight she would treat herself to some fish and chips and a bottle of cider, and no one would be the wiser.

CHAPTER ONE
ARRIVAL

It was nearing midday when the train finally pulled into the Temple Meads Station. John Bottrell sat by the smeared window, staring out at the great pillars of Isambard Kingdom Brunel's lofty edifice, and wished he were anywhere else but here, cocooned in this airless environment. The air was hot and fetid with the stale breath and reek of passengers' bodies, crammed into the narrow train compartment. Next to him a huge man with sagging jowls slumbered on, his head glistening with sweat, a trail of dribble inching its way down the side of his mouth. In front of him lay the desiccated remains of his British Rail meal: the crusts of a bleached corned beef sandwich, an empty packet of crisps and two crumpled cans of lager.

It was the summer of 1976. For nearly three months now he'd woken to blue cloudless skies and a sun which bore down on the London streets like a remorseless orange eye. Wherever he went that summer, the heat enclosed him. The pavements stank and were stained with hardened chewing gum, dog urine and from the roofs of houses, even at 7am, he could see the hot air rising, as if the city were some giant oven. And in the squad car, where he spent much of his day, he and his colleague slowly cooked like oven-ready chickens.

Over the course of the last three months he had assisted in four murder cases. He had begun to think it was due to the heat and the potentially explosive nature of man. As a graduate in criminology he had been placed on the fast track training scheme straight after leaving Hendon College. At Hendon his results had been described by a senior officer as 'outstanding'. It had therefore been suggested to him that he would be a suitable candidate for Special Branch, but he had discovered that his student membership of CND had precluded him from joining. Secretly, he was relieved at the ban since, as a lifelong liberal, he had no wish to be a mole for the state. Besides, there was the distinct possibility he might be posted to Northern Ireland, that tortured and divided outpost of British imperialism, as his father had once called it.

The murder squad had been headed by DCI Ian Glenister, a tall, granite-faced Glaswegian whose terse, clipped manner displayed his tough background. Glenister had been brought up in the Gorbals and came from the school of hard knocks. By the age of sixteen he had left school and entered the world of amateur boxing. By eighteen he was working the streets of his home town, busting junkies, pimps and gunrunners.

The wealth of experience which he had garnered over the next three years put him in a strong position when it came to promotion, and it was not long before he found his way south to the Smoke, as he fondly called it, enlisting as a DC with the Met. Two years later he found, rather to his surprise, that he had risen through the ranks to the exalted rank of Chief Inspector.

Glenister had called Bottrell 'the college boy with brains'. Bottrell was a walking encyclopedia of criminology. If Glenister wanted to know the finer points on strangulation technique, then it was John he asked, not the pathologist or SOCCO. There was a directness of purpose about John Bottrell which the older man warmed to. He absorbed knowledge like a sponge. Glenister admired that ability and the younger man's confidence, humility and honesty. Glenister rarely introduced him to staff at briefings. At the mortuary he would only refer to him as 'you' or 'he'.

And when the long day's work had finally concluded, it was Bottrell who fetched the older man his favourite malt whisky at the run-down bar in Compton St.

It came as no surprise, therefore, that when Glenister was instructed to set up the Special Investigations Unit in Bristol, in the spring of 1976, Bottrell had received the summons to join him.

The passengers started to file out of the carriage, a tired crowd, disgorging onto the platform. Their muted conversations were soon lost in the harsh blare of the tannoy. Bottrell, wincing at the strident noise, grabbed his case and followed the throng into the stifling heat of the station, past a small group of Hare Krishna acolytes, past the old GWR offices, with their limestone Tudor facades, until he finally reached the hustle and bustle of Victoria Street. Turning right, he paused to consult his map of the city, then made his way via Redcliffe Way, crossing the floating harbour and cutting across Queen Square.

It was midday now and the sun, directly overhead, beat down on him mercilessly, like a great arc lamp. The square was strewn with half naked office girls and male clerks in uncomfortable office clothes. Unable to stand the heat they had stripped to their waists, their white bodies already burnt from the intensity of the sun. They looked like bloated lobsters. The rest of the workers lay huddled in the shade of the few large trees. Around them the withered grass was littered with the debris of packed lunches.

He crossed the river again, making his way up to College Green. Every available patch of shade was crammed with students idly dipping into packed lunches or drowsing sleepily in the heat. He was sweating profusely now and stopping every so often to catch his breath and glance at the map. Past the great crescent of offices and up into Park Street until at last he turned left into Great George Street. Number 27 was his destination.

A tall, red-brick Georgian villa, once built to house a wealthy Bristol merchant, it now served as the headquarters of the Avon and Somerset Police's Special Investigations Unit. He climbed the worn limestone steps and pressed the intercom. From the direction of Park Street the roar of the distant traffic echoed up into the quiet, tree-lined road. To his left he could see the edge of Brandon Hill and the tip of Cabot Tower. Down the road, ambling and chatting, a group of female students, dressed in bright, flared trousers and lurid T-shirts, made their way back to the university. As they passed, Bottrell noticed the familiar acrid odour of a joint, which wafted up through the still air.

A voice, harsh and businesslike, cut through his reverie.

"Yes, who is it?"

"DC John Bottrell. I have an appointment with DCI Glenister, Special Investigations Unit."

The intercom buzzed noisily and he pushed it open, finding himself in a long hallway. It looked more like a hotel lobby than a police building, he thought, as he took in the Victorian furniture and an elaborate glass chandelier. The ceiling was exquisite. He made his way up the stairs to the first floor where a plain brown door was marked 'Special Investigations Unit'.

Inside, two men sat either side of a low table. One of them he recognised instantly as Glenister. Fundamentally he had not changed since their last encounter in the Met, except he had lost more hair from around his greying temples. But there was no disguising the thin, pock-marked, aquiline face, and the grey flesh of the inveterate smoker. Glenister stood up and smiled. He was dressed in a tired-looking grey suit and the most hideous tie Bottrell had seen. He felt distinctly nauseous.

"Bottrell! Good to see you again!" Glenister exclaimed. "Good journey?"

"More like the black hole of Calcutta, but I made it," he replied. "This is DC Mike Evans. Ex Gower police. He and I are old sparring partners. Go back a long way."

The other man stood up, a burly, dark haired Welshman with a broken nose who looked as if he could take care of himself in a tight corner.

"Nice to meet you." His accent was very strong. Cardiff, Bottrell guessed. "Ian's told me a lot about you."

"None of it good, I can assure you," Glenister joked. "Fixed up your digs yet?"

"I have a flat. In fact, it's my mother's. Going over there this afternoon to have a look."

"You're set up then, and ready to go. Grab yourself a cup of gnat's piss, give us ten minutes and I'll show you round." He pointed to the coffee machine in the corner.

Bottrell sprawled in a large leather chair by the window. The tall room, lined with grey filing cabinets and makeshift bookshelves, seemed incongruously untidy in such elegant surroundings. Rolling up his sleeves he stood up and went over to the window. To his right he could see the great green mound of Brandon Hill, shimmering in the heat, and to his left the dense grey fug of the traffic as it made its way down Park Street. He had not been in Bristol for at least fifteen years. Of course, much was the same. He remembered his mother taking him to the museum with its imposing Edwardian portico, and being fascinated by its collection of stuffed animals. His enquiring mind had wondered at the fossilised remains of prehistoric

23

creatures and he had delighted at the Romany caravan. It was this same enquiring mind which had led him to his present path.

But there was much that had changed in this great city. It was more polluted now. Amid the imposing Victorian monuments, ugly concrete blocks had mushroomed, marring the sweep of the city landscape. In the intense summer heat the city seemed to be choking from the sheer weight of people and traffic.

"Admiring the view?"

He turned to find Glenister bearing a cup of steaming coffee. Next to him stood a tall young woman with large eyes and luxurious, long blonde hair.

"This is Dr Frances Leadbetter. She's our psychologist."

Bottrell extended his left hand in greeting.

"Pleased to meet you. I'm John Bottrell."

"From Bristol?"

"How did you guess?"

She smiled, a broad, cat-like smile, her dark eyes glinting at him.

"Your accent. It gives you away, I'm afraid."

"Dr Leadbetter has made a study of human behaviour," Glenister observed wryly. "It's what she does for a living. She provides us with the human dimension. That's why she's part of the team."

"I was also raised in Bristol. Redland, to be precise."

"Really?"

"Redland Girls School, then Bristol University."

"Excuse me for butting in, won't you, but I'd like to talk shop for a wee while." There was a trace of irritation in Glenister's voice. Unphased by this interruption she flashed a grin at him. What an attractive woman, Bottrell thought.

She had a small, petite mouth and her high cheekbones and smooth skin gave her a slightly continental look. Pulling himself together Bottrell followed the others through a set of double doors to a large, airy room, lit by harsh neon lights.

"Our centre of operations," Glenister proudly announced. "Over here, the latest in forensic hardware and here, a fully operational laboratory."

Bottrell cast an eye over the equipment. There was a mortuary table, high-powered microscopes, projection screen and OHPs. He was impressed.

"How big is the team?" he asked.

"Just the four of us. DC Dave Thomas you haven't met yet. He's over in Paris, following up a lead on our case."

"Oh yes?"

"Yes, DC Evans will fill you in on the details. Let's go next door where we can have a smoke, shall we?"

Next door Evans was waiting for them in front of a display board, arrayed with a series of photographs. They showed a red bricked building set in an overgrown garden. Picking up a cane pointer, he cleared his throat and began, his rich Welsh baritone booming. Bottrell sat on the sofa opposite.

"About ten days ago," Evans began, "the residents of 10, Woodfield Road, decided to tidy up their garden. They'd recently purchased the property which, up until then, had been rented out to students. Mary and George Talbot were aware that the property had an ice house, but when the agent had shown them round prior to purchase, no one had thought of examining it properly. On 4th July, the wife had been cutting the grass when she decided to look inside. That's when she discovered the remains of our Jane Doe." He pointed to an enlarged photo showing what appeared to be a bundle of clothes from the centre of which extended a skeletal hand.

"Dr Linklater, the pathologist, estimated that the remains were that of a woman in her mid-thirties. She had probably lain there for a period of four years and had died sometime in the summer. He found evidence of at least two stab wounds, one which had serrated a bone in the rib cage, the other which had severed the spinal column in the lumbar region. There were also minute remains of tape across the mouth, suggesting the victim may have been gagged immediately prior to her death. Although the clothes were much decayed, he was able to show she had been wearing a white coat. From the remains of the label inside it would appear the coat was of French design. All identifying papers and possessions were absent, probably removed by her assailant. One of her shoes was missing, probably lost elsewhere. Perhaps the actual attack had taken place somewhere else... nearby perhaps? The murderer may have dragged the body into the ice house, hoping it would not be found for some time. What else? Oh yes. She had had a considerable amount of dentistry done but as yet her dental records haven't been traced. We also checked the missing persons list for the years in question, but as yet, nothing."

"DC Thomas has interviewed most of the local residents but that hasn't yielded anything of interest. Reason being that most of them weren't even there five years ago. Besides which, at least three of the adjoining houses are rented to university students, so that line of investigation is pretty hopeless," Glenister observed.

"However, the coat has been of some use to us. It's an unusual make apparently, sold only in a handful of Parisian fashion houses. Hence DC Thomas's visit to Paris. At least two of these posh clothes shops supply goods to their customers on an account basis, so we're keeping our fingers crossed. We're also conducting a search in the missing persons bureau run by the Sûreté," Evans added.

"What about local hotels, B&Bs, guest houses etc.?" asked Bottrell.

"Good point. Too wide a remit I'm afraid. Trouble is, the pathologist can only estimate the death to within a few weeks. There wasn't much left of her I'm afraid. Plus the summer is a pretty busy period for foreign tourists in the Bristol area. There's also an additional complication because there are at least three foreign language schools who accommodate French students during the summer and they all lie within a one mile radius of Woodfield Road. No, our best bet is the coat and the Paris connection."

The phone rang and Glenister picked it up straight away. After a succession of monosyllabic answers he replaced the receiver.

"What's up?" Evans asked.

"We'll have to suspend this meeting. Sorry about that. Bodies of two males found walled up in a house in the St Paul's area. The attending DC thinks it might be a gangland homicide. I think Evans and I will look at this one. Perhaps you could entertain John here for a while, Dr Leadbetter? In fact..." He picked up his diary and turned the pages.

"I won't really be needing you both until tomorrow morning."

He scribbled a note on a piece of paper, then handed it to Bottrell.

"Meet us at this address. 9am tomorrow morning, sharp, will you?"

When they had gone Bottrell and Frances made their way down Charlotte Street into Park Street where they found an Italian coffee house. Over black coffees they chatted for a while,

Bottrell finding they had much in common. They even shared the same birth month. He sat sipping his coffee, listening to her talk about her childhood in Bristol, but although he nodded and made dutiful replies, he found that he was not really listening. He found himself staring at the soft down on the nape of her neck as she turned to speak to him, her rich, full bodied blonde hair and the occasional faint blush to her cheeks as she became aware of his gaze. There was an intensity of manner about her which he found rare in the other women he had come across. He had had relationships with probably half a dozen women over the last six years, yet not one of them had that combination of intellectual strength and conviction that he found in Frances. By the time they had left, he found, rather to his surprise, that he had invited her for a drink that evening.

It took him a while to find the estate agents in Wells Road. The afternoon heat had reached critical mass and he found he was having to stop in his tracks every so often to regain his breath. Keys and Rowlands were situated on the second floor of a tall Victorian building and after he had negotiated the narrow stairs, he was almost completely exhausted and bathed in sweat. A tall, angular-jawed man in a cheap suit and heavy Buddy Holly glasses welcomed him to Bristol and gave both commiserations for his mother's death and the keys to her flat. Soon he was out onto the busy street.

He was familiar with the route to the flat, having explored just about every inch of the city on his bike when he was young. In those days the family had lived in a large villa in Oakfield Road, close to the university, where his father worked as a lecturer. His mother had been a part-time librarian. The road was still busy with students, many of them weaving their way through the traffic on rusting bicycles, long hair drifting behind them in the breeze.

Halfway along Pembroke Road he found No 10, a grand Victorian building, set back from the road by a tall yew tree hedge. It seemed grimier and more run-down than he had imagined it when he last visited his mother. Looking at the battered front door and hearing the noise which drifted down from the upper floors, it appeared that several of the flats had been rented out to the more rowdy elements of the student population.

He glanced at the names: J & K Beddoes, R Deacon. K Smith, A Bottrell... He winced. The estate agent had not even bothered to remove his mother's name from the door. But then why would they? She had only been dead a month. He remembered his last visit. She had been a frail shadow of her former self and had lain back on the pillows, her face grey, her cheeks emaciated from the cancer that had eaten away at her. They had treated her with great care at the Bristol General Infirmary but Anne Bottrell had always believed in alternative medicine. She had believed she could beat the disease which finally engulfed her by the power of positive thinking and prayer. A devoted Christian spiritualist all her life, she was herself a medium and her son had inherited her ability to sense things from the shadowy land of the spirits. As he grew older he learned to keep this side of his nature from his friends and colleagues.

Nevertheless he had found this 'talent' useful in his police career. Glenister would have been appalled if he had known.

The passageway of No 10 smelt of stale vegetables and its scuffed walls were evidence of neglect. He sighed. Behind Flat 2's door he could hear a child crying and a woman's voice raised in anger. He climbed the threadbare stairs, pausing for breath on the first landing. Most of the flats seemed poorly maintained. On the second landing he paused, hearing the sound of voices from below. He peered down the stairwell and glimpsed two women. The first, a short, squat girl in her mid-twenties, was chatting amicably to a second, dark haired girl on the stairs.

He continued to climb to the top. Unlocking the door, he paused, perhaps fearing the ghosts of his own past would be waiting for him. When the family solicitor had explained the terms of his mother's will, he had not been surprised that she had left him the flat. After all, his younger sister now lived in Canada and his older brother had died in a motorbike accident while on holiday in Scotland, some two years before his mother's illness. He had always wondered if the news of Hugh's death had precipitated the onset of her cancer. He suddenly felt very alone.

Inside, the early afternoon sun was streaming in from the living room, casting streaks of yellow across the great Jacobean oak sideboard and the hat stand where his father would always hang his jacket and coat. Nothing here had really changed. There was a stale, dusty smell but at least the flat was in better condition than he thought. Throwing open the windows he breathed in as much of the air as he could. What a view from up here.

He was about to make his way into the kitchen when he heard a soft knock at the door. There he found the young woman from the hallway.

"So sorry to disturb you," she said, smiling.

"I apologise but I must ask for your help," she continued. "I am from Flat 5 across the hallway."

She had a strong French accent but her English was very good.

"Yes?" he said.

"Forgive me, my English is not good."

"No, it's fine, go ahead."

"I am locked out. I have this key but it does not open the door. Can you help me?"

She smiled again, revealing a set of large, white teeth. She extended her hand in greeting.

"I am Anne Marie. You see the problem," she continued, showing him the key.

"No, not really, but let's have a look at the lock," he replied.

He moved past her and inserted the key into the lock, then jiggled it back and forth, but the door refused to budge. He tried again, this time with greater force. The door shifted half an inch. He put his shoulder to it and the door gave. He stood in the doorway, grinning at her.

"There we are. Just a bit stiff. I'll oil it for you. My name's John. John Bottrell. As you can see I've just moved in. This was my mother's flat. I guess we're next door neighbours."

"You are so kind. So kind. Please do come in. I shall make us some coffee."

He stepped inside, thanking her. The flat was smaller than his own. There was a smell of rosemary in the room, as if she had been using an incense burner.

"Please do sit down. Black or white?" she asked.

"Black please. No sugar."

"You smoke?" She offered him a French cigarette but he politely refused.

"So, which part of France are you from then?" he asked when she returned carrying two steaming mugs of coffee.

"I am from Paris. I am teaching French to students at the University," she explained. "This is my last term here. In August I must return home."

"How do you find Bristol?"

She frowned.

"This was easy. I used a map."

"No, no," he laughed. "Let me put it a different way. Do you like living here?"

She laughed, realising her mistake.

"Of course. I see. No. I like it very well. It is a most exciting city. The people are very kind here. Even the young woman downstairs. She has been very friendly. She helped me a great deal when I moved in to the flat. You said this was your mother's flat?"

"It was. She died a little while ago. I inherited it from her."

"I am so sorry. I had not realised."

"That's OK. You weren't to know."

"And what do you do – what is your job, John?"

"Actually, I'm a policeman. A detective."

"How exciting!"

"Sometimes. Not always. I used to work in London but I've come back home. Back to the city where I belong."

Anne Marie took the mugs into the kitchen.

"I won't be long," she said.

There was a sound at the front door. He stood up and peered round the door. The young, squat woman he had seen before in the stairwell, stood uncomfortably in the doorway. She was plainly dressed. A grubby white T-shirt bore the words 'The Who' across her chest. Bottrell smiled to himself. What it was to be young, he thought.

"I'm Katherine. I just came up to see if Anne Marie was alright." She struggled to erase her strong Bristol accent. Bottrell felt sorry for her obvious insecurity.

"I'm John Bottrell," he said kindly, "I've just moved in here. Anne Marie won't be a minute."

"Oh, alright." she said shyly. "I'll leave you to it then,"

She turned, and before he could answer her, made her way back down the stairs.

.

When Anne Marie had returned they sat and chatted for a while. She told him she had lived in the flat for the best part of a year on an exchange basis with an academic from the English Department at the university. Katherine and her husband had lived in the downstairs flat for about two years. They had bought it cheaply, transforming it from its semi-derelict state to its present bijou condition. When she arrived from Paris to take up her teaching post, Katherine had been most kind to her. On those days when her husband wasn't working, she had shown Anne Marie the sights of the city and she had soon gained a thorough knowledge of the museums and art galleries. Katherine had a three month old baby but she had never seen it. They very rarely took it out because it had been born prematurely and was physically disabled.

They continued to chat for about an hour then he thanked Anne Marie and returned to his mother's flat. He washed and changed into fresh clothes, then locked the flat and made his way out into the baking heat of Pembroke Road.

CHAPTER TWO
HEAT

She had spotted the knife in a small shop off Park Street. It was one of those places which sold militaria, its windows protected by a strong, vandal-proof iron mesh. She had often passed the place on her way to work but on this occasion she paused and stood staring for a few moments before entering the dingy interior of the shop.

When she got home she sat in the kitchen examining her purchase. Described by the shop owner as a bowie knife, it had a long bone handle and curved blade. She placed the point of the knife against her wrist and slowly began to apply pressure. There was a sharp pain and a trickle of blood began to ooze from her pale skin. But she didn't seem to feel the pain. She was thinking of her mother and the dark cupboard where she had been incarcerated. She looked down. A pool of crimson had collected on the Formica table. Putting down the knife, she got up and searched for a plaster in the kitchen drawer. A shaft of sunlight fell on the gleaming blade. She picked it up again. The handle was warm to the touch, warmer than flesh itself. It would serve her purpose well.

She returned to the kitchen window. She needed to watch. Stand guard. It was essential she knew everything that was happening. So she stood like a sentinel…

* * *

Bottrell looked at his watch. Five o'clock already. He would have ample time to make his way down to the harbour to meet Frances at the Llandogger Inn. He pushed his way past a large group of foreign students who were blocking the pavement. They were talking in animated voices and jostling each other outside a tall, stuccoed building bearing the inscription 'Belmont Language School'. Half of them appeared to be French and German, the others were possibly of Asian and Middle Eastern origin.

He was glad he had not taken the bus down into the city centre, for a strong breeze had sprung up, lifting the barrier of heat from his face.

He had taken off his jacket and was walking swiftly along the edge of the pavement, past the tall, imposing villas of Queen's Road, heading for Park Street. As he drew level with the Wills Memorial building, a group of students holding placards, approached him and handed him a leaflet bearing the symbol of CND. He glanced at it, then thrust it into his pocket. The city seemed alive, more so than when he had lived here as a youth. Whether it was the hot weather or the number of students, he wasn't sure, but there was a buzz to the streets which made him feel alive.

Small groups of youths lay on College Green, soaking up the sun, some smoking and drinking from cans. He could hear the choir rehearsing in the Cathedral, their voices wafting up, echoing from inside the great perpendicular tower. The air was cooling rapidly now, the sun just tipping the roofs of the surrounding buildings. Soon the streets would be tranquil and shady.

He wove his way down in the direction of the harbour, heading for the inn, thinking of the tall, graceful Frances Leadbetter, for whom he had felt an immediate and quite irrational attraction as soon as he had seen her. Eyes that were deep and soulful, her long face framed by golden hair. During their brief encounter at the office they had passed only a few words, yet in that short time, he had sensed she too had felt something. Careful, he told himself. Not too quickly off the diving board. The water may be colder than you think.

As he made his way to the inn he spotted her. She was sitting at one of the plastic tables by the harbour side, sipping a long drink. Dressed in a long black loose jacket and matching short skirt, she looked stunning. And when she turned and waved to him, he threw caution to the wind.

* * *

She had spotted them on College Green, a group of about twenty students clustered around a park bench. As she walked by on the other side, she could hear from their accents that at least half a dozen of them were French. She smiled in anticipation. One in particular caught her attention: a tall, thin, pale faced girl with short, black hair. She was sitting on the edge of the circle, looking rather left out of things, not saying very much. She walked into a sandwich bar and bought herself a cheese and onion roll, then crossed the road and sat for a while on a bench about fifty yards away, watching them as she ate. She always felt so hungry at this point. After a while the crowd drifted down into St George's Road, clutching their cans, some arm in arm, the dark haired girl at the rear, looking awkward and walking alone.

She followed at a discreet distance, walking casually, knowing that this was important, to be present but invisible to

36

passers-by. Fortunately the streets were quiet by now and the sun had all but disappeared over the roof tops, casting her into shadow. She was wearing mirrored sunglasses and the black wig she always kept in her bag, just in case.

On the corner of York Place the group gathered, then said their goodbyes, leaving a small crowd of half a dozen who made their way down towards the harbour side. The dark haired girl stood for a moment, deliberating, then followed them. They stopped at the Llandogger Inn, sitting down at the tables outside, while a few of their number went inside to order.

She decided she would follow suit, ordering herself a lager, then find a seat by the door. She had a perfect view of the harbour and the group outside.

The bar was not crowded at this early hour and she knew she would hardly be noticed.

Outside, a few couples sat drinking and chatting, relieved at the coolness of the air. She lit a cigarette and took her time over her drink, hoping the students would soon disperse, but when two of them returned to the bar to order more drinks, she knew it would be a test of her patience. Whatever she did, she must keep a clear head. She had finished her second cigarette and was about to return to the bar, when she heard a babble of voices from the Harbour side. Peering through the gap in the doorway, she realised that some of the company were about to go. Picking up her bag she glanced quickly round the bar. Good. No one was paying her the slightest attention.

The company ambled along, the girl walking slowly at the rear. All alone. Finally the students split up, the dark haired girl walking quickly now up towards Brandon Hill. She seemed glad to be away from them. Her watcher felt a pang of sympathy for this outsider. How well she knew that feeling. Old anger threatened to surface but she pushed it down swiftly. She was close to her now, about forty yards behind her. The only other occupant of the park was an elderly woman with a white stick and a small Yorkshire terrier. As she approached, the dog suddenly leapt up at her and began to claw at her skirt. She stepped back, caught momentarily off balance. The woman at once intervened, tugging at the dog's lead.

"Hubert, come here, stop that immediately! I'm so sorry. I hope he hasn't hurt you?"

"It's no problem. No damage done. I'm fine. Really."

"Well I'm really sorry. I'm afraid you're offended."

The girl pushed past her and the dog roughly, aware of the woman's scrutiny. But she had no time for this. She had spent too long here already. She quickened her pace. Where was the girl? Curse the dog and the woman. She must *not* lose her now. Then she saw her. She was at least a hundred yards ahead now and making swift progress towards the summit of Brandon Hill. Soon the path would enter a clump of trees. If she was quick and closed the gap, she would not be seen from the rest of the hill. She was almost running now in an effort to catch up.

She glanced back. The old woman had disappeared. There was no one else about. She must take her chance now or the moment would be lost. She reached the fork in the path and spotted the girl about twenty yards to her left. She had stopped to look up at the tall beech trees, whose leaf laden branches were thrown into shadow.

About ten yards away, she stopped to regain her composure, then called out:

"Excuse me! Excuse me! I don't suppose you've got a light?"

She knew this would work. She had seen her smoking on the harbour side. The young woman turned, startled by the interruption, then began to turn back towards her, smiling. She reached into her bag and brought out a packet of cigarettes, her hand skimming the edge of the cold blade. The young woman reached into her pocket and produced a silver lighter.

"Lovely evening, isn't it?" she said calmly, stepping closer.

"Beautiful. Very fine," the young woman replied. She spoke with a soft accent. Another French girl. Close up she noticed her beautiful hazel eyes and soft skin. So soft, she was just like the doll she had been given for her sixth birthday. Why was she so beautiful? It wasn't fair. Her resentment flooded through her like a tidal wave.

"Are you a visitor?" she asked briskly, trying to control her anger.

"Student."

"You live here?"

"Yes, I live here."

"If you go to the top of that tower you can see right over the city," she said pointing to the Cabot Tower.

The young student replaced her lighter in her pocket and turned to look up at the tower. The knife slid out of her pocket so easily. She stepped forward and plunged it into the young woman's back, drawing it out again quickly. It was important to get the angle right. The less blood the better. The young woman staggered, then turned, her face a mask of pain and bewilderment. Stepping sideways, she raised the knife, then drove it into her chest, aiming for the heart. She stepped back quickly. The young woman reached out, then reeled back, choking, keeling over onto her back, her eyes glazing.

She looked about her. There was still no one about. The footpath was clear. She couldn't believe her luck. Donning a pair of surgical gloves she began dragging the victim off the path. To her left was a small hut used by council gardeners and next to it a large enclosed area for garden refuse, half-filled with discarded cuttings. She pulled with all her might, twisting her burden this way and that in an effort to gain momentum. Still half-conscious, the young French woman moaned softly. She got the body into the compound, then knelt down amongst the debris. Reaching into her bag she pulled out a roll of tape and twisted it firmly round the woman's mouth. Looking down at the pale face she leant forward, stroked the woman's face once, then snipped off a section of the smooth, dark hair. Then she stood up and, steadying herself for a moment, slowly removed her bloodstained jacket and the surgical gloves, thrusting them into her bag. She looked down at her skirt. There was a spattering of bloodstains around her waist and thighs but she hoped they would not be noticed. She had tried hard to avoid spillage. What a nuisance.

"Not so much of a beauty now, are we? Non." Her laughter was cold and cruel.

Then she returned to the path, noting the thin trail of blood. She shrugged her shoulders, stopping only by the WC to remove the wig and glasses and check her make-up. Then she followed the footpath over the northern side of the hill, dropping down into the main street, where she was soon lost in the evening rush.

CHAPTER THREE
THE QUICKENING

She loathed the summer. She hated the long days of uninterrupted light it brought, the way it revealed and defined. She loathed its stark, merciless quality. In such a season nothing could be concealed, no secrets remained hidden. Everything was laid bare. There were no hiding places. And this summer, with its harsh, sun-drenched days and suffocating heat, was worse than most.

She longed for the dark of winter, when the days were shortest and a pale sun rode in the heavens, often obscured by cloud. Even then she walked in shadow. And at night, when the moon shone through her bedroom window, she placed a shield over her eyes, to shut out the disturbing silver light that threatened to disturb her dreams. There were no mirrors in her bedroom, nor in the hall, the lounge, not even the bathroom. There was no place she could glimpse her own image, for to her true self she was invisible. She had become part of the shadow land. There, she could walk unseen, unobserved by others, her secret life safe from prying eyes.

It had not always been like this. As a small child she had loved the sunlight, played on the beach like others of her age, stared up at the blue sky and wondered at its infinity. Yet, as time passed and she learned to defend herself, she had gathered the darkness into her being and the world of light had slipped slowly away until, at last, the darkness had claimed her for its own. Now she took sustenance from its strength. It was a wellspring of her power. It was her guide and counsellor.

By the age of twelve, she had found her inner sanctum, a retreat where she could sit alone in the darkness, the only time in her beleaguered life when she could feel utterly secure. It lay in the small copse at the back of their house. She had discovered it purely by chance one summer morning when she had escaped the rambling red-brick house and found an area of wasteland which lay adjacent to a disused playing field. The area had been vacant and overgrown since the end of the war. Tall brambles and gorse bushes vied for space here, with spindly sycamores and ancient beech trees.

There was a track through the woods. Marked by a broken footpath sign, it was rarely used by locals but in the spring it harboured a rich crop of bluebells. Here it was, half-concealed by a pile of rotting leaves, that she discovered the derelict Nissen hut. Through that long autumn that followed it had become her refuge, a place where she could recover from the iron hand of her mother. She would sit in the stillness, listening only to the sounds of birds, bound by the security and safety of its lichen-covered walls.

Here it was that she learned to embrace the dark until it became her source, her wellspring of power. She would lie back on the pile of old newspapers and blanket she had smuggled out of the house and imagine her mother's death a hundred times, in a hundred different ways.

Then, one day, in late July, something terrible had happened. Her secret was discovered. She had gone to the hut in the late morning, slipping out of the back door to escape her mother. At this time of the year the waste ground had grown dense and luxuriant and the hut itself was almost totally obscured by tall ferns, but she had cleared a space by the entrance where the morning sunlight penetrated the foliage of the surrounding trees. She had taken to sunbathing here, tentatively at first, but after a couple of occasions when no one came by, her confidence had grown and she had removed her clothes and lain naked in the hot sun.

On this particular morning she had been lying like this, her eyes closed, trying to shut out the thoughts that haunted her, when she became aware of a sound. Looking up, she saw a figure behind the beech tree to the left of the hut. She sat up, starting to gather her clothes, hurriedly trying to dress herself, but it was too late. In a moment a man had stepped from behind the tree. He said something incomprehensible to her, then lunged at her. She had pushed him away and had attempted to stand, but he was on her in an instant. A tall, wasted figure, probably a vagrant, his clothes stank of urine. His face was grey and covered in white stubble and when he pressed his mouth to hers, his breath reeked of alcohol. She tried to scream but he pressed his hand tightly over her mouth and she did not have the strength to resist him. The fear and the subsequent pain was too much to bear.

After it was over and he had disappeared into the trees, she lay on the ground, shaking with anger, weeping with pain. Then she dressed herself and made her way slowly back home. Her mother had shouted at her, demanding to know why she was so late and demanding to know where she had been but she had said nothing, not daring to share her secret, preferring instead to receive the blows that rained on her back and head, suffering the cruel punishment in abject silence. When the beating was over, she showered, then retreated to her bedroom, trying to shut out the pictures in her mind, struggling to obliterate his face and the smell of his body. But the pictures persisted. The tears had long gone. All that remained was the deep, intense anger that filled her like a black cloud. Over the years the anger had grown like a cancer within her.

* * *

Glenister stood staring at the opening in the plasterboard. Inside, covered by plaster dust, lay two figures, their legs askew, their arms intertwined as if they were lovers, locked in an incongruous embrace. Although both were long dead, their clothes had survived. One was dressed in a long, garishly coloured kaftan, the other in cheap cotton trousers and a very faded yellow T-shirt. For some reason, whether it was the gap in the floorboards below them or their proximity to the loft, the air had mummified their bodies. The skin was dry and wrinkled like old leather, stretched tight and thin across their bones.

"So what have we got?" Glenister asked the tall, dome-headed pathologist who stood beside him. He was peering down at the bodies with complete detachment. He was something like a cadaver himself, mused Bottrell. The latter knew him well, having trained under him at Bristol University. An emotionless man who spoke with a pronounced Edinburgh accent, he, like Glenister, had come from a tough, working class background. Having achieved a scholarship, he had endured the rigours of a Jesuit education before entering the exalted ranks of Oxford University where he had pioneered advances in bloodstain identification.

"Like to comment, young John?" he asked, a twinkle in his eye. At Bristol, Walker or 'Dougie' as he was affectionately known, had been renowned for his unorthodox methods. He would create an imaginary crime scene in his rooms and invite his students to comment on what they could discover from the evidence, setting them a strict time limit, then awarding them marks for their relative progress. During such sessions he would say absolutely nothing to them but he would stand in the corner of the room and scribble furiously on his notepad. It was an unnerving teaching technique but one which yielded remarkable results.

Bottrell knelt down and, donning a pair of gloves, cast a cursory eye over the emaciated bodies.

"Both were tortured prior to death," he said at last. "There are several cigarette burns. And they almost certainly had their hands bound before death. See here, these contusion marks about the wrists. This one," he said, kneeling down again and indicating with his forefinger, "has been attacked from behind by what was probably a long bladed knife. See here, the cut extends from high up near the ear and sweeps down across the front of the throat, then back up on the opposite side. The movement is from left to right."

"Indicating?" asked Walker.

"That the assailant was right handed."

"Excellent," commented Walker, looking pleased.

"This second victim may or may not have been killed by the same attacker," Bottrell said. "And the weapon is not the same either. There are two major wounds here, both in the upper rib cage. Both wounds are deep and wedge shaped, suggesting an axe or meat cleaver. If you look at the shape of the rib bones you'll see they've been fractured by the force of the blows. And there's one more thing. There's evidence around the mouths of both victims of fibres and a gluey, resinous substance. I couldn't swear to it but I'd say it's a fair bet that they had their mouths taped up before they were killed. What else? Both males, both aged in their mid-twenties, both Afro Caribbean. And both carry

45

a small tattoo on the left forearm. Bit indistinct. Can't make it out. Probably been here several years."

"And kiln-dried to perfection, by the look of them," Walker observed. "Well done John. You've missed very little of significance, which is only what I would have expected of you. However, let me add a little light and shade while we're at it. This one here, for example, has a number of his front teeth missing. There's also an old stab wound on his neck. I'm surprised you didn't notice that. It would indicate a fairly violent lifestyle, prior to his untimely death. The second victim also kept a dog with which he was probably on very friendly terms, An Alsatian I should say, looking at the length and colour of the hairs. There is more, but I won't bore you with the details." When he had finished, a loud clapping began from the corner of the room.

"Congratulations, gentlemen. That was most entertaining," said Glenister, dryly.

"But what about motive?" asked Evans, who had been hovering uncomfortably by the door.

"My bet is it's a revenge killing," Glenister replied. "What information do we have about the premises?" he asked a fresh-faced uniformed PC who had been standing outside in the corridor.

"Up until a year ago they were bedsits. The landlords were an outfit called City Lets, main office in West Street, Bedminster. They sold the property last year to the present owner, an Asian businessman. He owns a couple of restaurants in North Road."

"So who made the discovery?" Glenister asked.

"A couple of workmen. They were converting the rooms into a studio flat."

"How confident are we in getting a fix on when they were murdered?"

"Shouldn't be too difficult," the pathologist acknowledged. "I'll let you know once my examination has been completed."

"OK. We're done here just for now. By the way, has anyone seen Dr Leadbetter yet?"

Bottrell looked away, trying to conceal his mild embarrassment. The last he had seen of Frances had been around 2am that morning when he had left her flat in Alma Road. After the rendezvous by the harbour side they had returned for what was intended to be a quick nightcap but which, in fact, turned out to be something much more intimate. Fortunately his alarm clock had woken him at 6am, but he felt distinctly groggy, if somewhat elated at the memory of the previous evening.

As they made their way out into Bedminster Parade, the uniformed PC, who was now standing by Glenister's old Jaguar, said, "Message for you, sir," and he handed the car phone to him. Glenister listened for a few moments, making perfunctory noises, then turned and said, "We'll have to go. There's been a body of a young girl found on Brandon Hill. Oh, if Dr Leadbetter turns up, let her know where we are, will you, constable?"

* * *

Henry Bunce was a tall, heavily built man of middle years whose twin passions in life were gambling and Australian lager. It was rare that he ever began work before 9am. His assistant, a lean, black youth called Maurice Winston, was also late to work that day, having spent the previous evening finishing an exceptionally fine packet of ganja weed in his flat. By the time both men arrived at the gardeners' hut behind Cabot Tower, neither was particularly communicative, taking refuge in their coffee and tabloids. Bunce was the first to discover the body. Having cleared a quantity of fallen leaves from behind the water fountain, he had backed the pickup into the compound and had started sweeping out the load when a flash of white caught his eye. He turned the engine off and, climbing out of the driver's compartment, peered into the pile of fallen leaves. There was no doubt about it. He was staring at a human arm. Grabbing a broom from the back of the truck, he approached it tentatively, poking at the arm, then used the head of the broom to clear away the leaves. Within seconds a face appeared like a white mask, framed by dark hair. Blank eyes stared back at him. The mouth was tightly bound and from beneath the tape ran a ribbon of congealed blood.

Bunce drew back in horror. Dropping the broom, he made his way back to the gardener's hut, shouting Winston's name. When both men returned to the compound, they stood in silence, staring at the broken body of the French student. At last Bunce spoke.

"Best not to move her. Best we phone the police."

Winston turned, retching into the bushes.

* * *

The large walk-in cupboard had been an added bonus. When she had lived in the house in Redland there had been nowhere she could keep her precious mementoes or 'trophies' as she often thought of them. The cupboard was ideal. Six feet square, it was lined with shelves. She could walk right in, into that dark sanctuary where the sound was easily muffled by a stout oak door with a mortise lock. In this cupboard she kept her precious pieces: things found, things collected, each possessing some significance to her past. There were the small pebbles she had collected as a child at Barrow beach; the large doll with the brown eyes she had used as a poppet to work her magic on Rachel Hibbert, the class bully; the news cuttings from the *Bristol Evening Post*, giving detailed accounts of her first two victims, Sandra Hayes and Hazel Blicken; the battered bamboo cane stick her mother had used to beat her; a crumpled certificate for the short story prize she had won when she had been in the third year. She had been awarded this by Miss Dunstan, her English teacher. Miss Dunstan was a tall, willowy woman in her mid-twenties, with large, pendulous breasts and long blonde hair which she used to wear in a bun. She had taken an instant liking to her Miss Dunstan. In fact, she was besotted with her and her love of the subject was merely a reflection of her obsession. As a result of this, by the age of thirteen she had read all of Wordsworth, Keats and Shelley and was fast becoming acquainted with the entire works of Shakespeare. She became a willing acolyte, staring longingly in adoration and never failing to answer all Miss Dunstan's questions, much to the disgust and resentment of the other girls.

Her hopes were somewhat dashed when, one Saturday afternoon in early July, she was invited to a poetry reading with two other girls at Miss Dunstan's house in Redland. It was a very satisfying afternoon, with tea and sandwiches and shared readings from their favourite poets. But in the middle of the session a short, squat woman with cropped grey hair entered the room. She clearly shared the house with Miss Dunstan and the looks that passed between them made it quite clear to her that they were truly partners. The unpalatable truth came like a knife in her heart. She had left, weakly making her excuses.

Boys, she discovered in her late teens, were rough, uncouth and obsessed by only one thing. She became a passive receptacle for their unbridled lust, remaining cold and impervious to their touch, shutting herself away from the experience as she had done all those years before. But she could still see the tramp's face and smell his rank body. She equated the act of sex as another of those unpleasant bodily functions. The likelihood of finding another Miss Dunstan was too remote.

She put down her large handbag and, opening it, removed the bloodstained coat, smoothing it out on the pine table. It would have to be destroyed of course, she told herself. It was a pity, but there it was. She glanced round the room. There were other treasures here, things she had always kept secret from her husband. He was forbidden from entering this cupboard and he would never have dared to question her about it. He was afraid of her temper and her strength.

There was a collection of birds' bones, feathers and shells, pieces of road kill and fragments of predated animals she had found on woodland walks as a child. And then there was the fur. It had been cut from an old neighbour's cat. The woman had been an irritant to her, trying to undermine her position in the flats. She would have seen to the woman herself eventually, but she had strong allies in the house. So she had settled the score through the cat. She smiled in remembrance. All these mementoes of death were reminders of how universal death was. She called them 'the quickened ones', these small cadavers, for she believed that at the moment of death the spirits of the living were 'quickened', that they were in an exalted state.

At the far end of the cupboard she had built a kind of altar, fashioned from pieces of driftwood, and here she had lain out her flotsam and jetsam of wood and seashore; bones whitened and sculpted by winds and rain; wings of gulls, the foot of a rabbit, the skull of a sheep. And there were other things: a discarded, battered doll, rescued from her childhood, a tattered photo showing herself at the age of three, looking lost and bewildered on the beach at Weston-super-Mare, her old English exercise book with the prize-winning story in it she had written at the age of twelve and which her mother had tried to destroy by hurling it onto the fire in a drunken rage. She would sit in here, surrounded by her mementoes, listening to the silence that surrounded her, marshalling her fractured past, reliving every moment of her pain and fear, planning her acts of vengeance. And when it all became too much she would become so claustrophobic she would burst out of the house and roam the streets, seeking a way of releasing that hate and anger. When she crossed the threshold into that dark cupboard, she was able to gather her strength and sanity once again.

She opened her bag again and, reaching in, pulled out the plastic bag with its lock of dark hair, the hair she had cut from the body on Brandon Hill. Then she placed it on the altar next to the skulls and the birds' wings, next to the other lock of hair that had lain there for so many years. She sat back in the chair and closed her eyes, feeling the souls of the departed gathering in the room. She laughed. The quickening had begun.

* * *

By the time Glenister and the others reached the Cabot Tower on Brandon Hill, the sun was already beating down on them from a cloudless sky, so much so that Glenister had to stop every so often to catch his breath as he climbed the steep steps. Only Bottrell waited dutifully for him at the top of the steps, the others striding ahead to where the familiar red and white hazard tape flapped in the breeze, indicating the scene of the crime. Glenister coughed, cursed, then, regaining his composure, removed his jacket and caught up with his young assistant.

51

Bottrell, who walked in silence as Glenister made excuses about his excessive smoking, was in reflective mood. He had been remembering what happened after he had left Frances and returned to his flat in Pembroke Road.

He had arrived back at around 2.30am, slightly the worse for wear, but still high in spirits. He had entered the building quietly, aware of the fact that the downstairs lights were still on in the ground floor flats. Not bothering to wash, he had quickly undressed and slipped between the sheets, naked because of the intense heat. It must have been soon after 4.30am when he woke, conscious of a sound coming from beyond the open window of the bedroom. Donning his dressing gown, he looked down. A full moon had risen, casting its silver light on the park which lay beyond the rear garden of the house. In the centre of the grass was a small Victorian fountain, long since disused. The figure of a woman stood there, motionless, her back to him.

She was dressed in a long coat, which seemed incongruous for the night air was still warm. She appeared to be weeping, her shoulders hunched as if she bore some deep sorrow.

Instinctively he pushed up the heavy sash window and called out to her, asking if she needed help, but the woman ignored him. In fact she did not even turn round to acknowledge him. He remained at the window for at least another minute, waiting for her to respond, but she did not. All he heard were those long, sustained, involuntary sobs, a haunting sound which drifted up to him on the cool night air. He was about to withdraw from the window when he noticed a light had been switched on in the flat next to his. The young French woman he had met earlier that day, had also been disturbed by the sound. This was not some waking dream then, some nocturnal apparition. Had she heard him calling, perhaps? He turned and checked his alarm clock to establish the exact time but when he looked back the woman had vanished. He shut the window gently and returned to his bed where he lay awake for a long while until sleep finally overcame him.

CHAPTER FOUR
THE BODY ON THE HILL

They had reached the summit of Brandon Hill, Glenister pushing past Bottrell and striding towards the red hazard tape that marked the perimeter of the murder scene. Bottrell followed his colleague's lean, coughing form. Inside the compound stood two uniformed policemen, a photographer, the tall, angular pathologist, Doug Walker, and Frances Leadbetter, who turned and smiled at him. He smiled back at her, recalling the evening they had spent together.

"When was she discovered?" Glenister was asking, interrupting his reverie.

"Around 9.30 this morning. One of the gardeners found her. Spotted her arm sticking out of a pile of leaves. Judging by the position of the body and the disturbance in the earth here, I'd say she was dragged off the main path just over here," said Walker, pointing through some tall beech trees towards the main footpath which skirted the top of the hill. Glenister knelt down and, donning a pair of gloves, lifted back the edge of the girl's coat.

"Any sign of sexual molestation?"

"Not as far as I can tell."

"When did she die?"

"Late yesterday evening, judging by the onset of rigor mortis. Cause of death: a punctured lung. In fact, she's suffered several stab wounds, probably inflicted by a long-bladed knife, I would guess. Delivered with some force by someone who was probably a few inches shorter than her. She was taken by surprise I would think. But look here, around the mouth. Notice anything?"

Glenister and Bottrell knelt down to examine the young woman's mouth. The lips showed signs of abrasion.

"See this?" asked Walker. "Her attacker has taped up her mouth."

"Prior to death?"

"It's difficult to say. Probably used some type of duct tape. If you look closely, you'll see traces of the adhesive and fibres from the tape."

Bottrell stared at the white face. The sightless eyes stared blankly back at him. She was like some strange Ophelia, drifting in a pool of leaves.

"Her hair has been cut, look, just above the right ear."

"A trophy perhaps?" asked Glenister.

"Quite possibly," replied Walker.

"Was she carrying any identification?"

"Unfortunately she wasn't," said the pathologist, moving back to allow the photographer to take a close-up of the body in situ. "However, the clothes may be a clue. The coat she's wearing isn't of British manufacture. We think it may be of French design."

Whilst they had been talking Bottrell had been looking at the ground to the left of the compound and was now some twenty paces off and standing beneath the beech trees, looking thoughtful.

"Look over here but be careful where you tread," Bottrell instructed. The two men walked over to where he was kneeling.

"You see this? A disturbance in the earth. The bush has been flattened where the victim possibly fell backwards. And here, look, two footprints in the soft earth. Small shoe size, possibly a woman's, definitely a trainer. And over here, blood spots on the leaves of the rose bush. The attacker was left-handed. You see how this footprint is much deeper than the other?"

"Indicating that she put more weight on it, which means her left hand was holding the knife."

"Exactly."

Glenister beckoned to the photographer.

"Get a shot of this will you? Oh, and we'll need a cast done of the footprint too. Well spotted John."

By lunchtime the thermometer in the office had reached ninety degrees. Although every window in the building had been flung wide open, it appeared to have made little difference to the stifling humidity of the interior. With Glenister's team stood a small group of additional officers, most of whom had removed their jackets and ties. Glenister himself was standing tieless and in his shirt sleeves in front of the white board, bands of perspiration staining his back and armpits. Opposite him, slumped on the black leather sofa, sat Evans and Leadbetter. Perched on a tubular chair was Bottrell. Red-rimmed about the eyes he made a series of concentric whorls in his notebook as he attempted to focus his thoughts. He did his best to avoid Frances' gaze but her heady perfume drifted across to him and he found it difficult to concentrate. He pushed all thoughts of their night together out of his mind. It was hard.

"I hope you're following this, Bottrell?" Glenister remarked.

"Perfectly."

"As I was saying," the tall Scotsman continued, "I shall be assigning the major responsibility for the Bedminster killings to

DC Mike Evans here. We'll be hearing from Mike in a few minutes. I shall be taking charge of the Brandon Hill murder and of course I'll be continuing with the Cotham case. Regarding the Brandon Hill business, since we have no immediate clues as to the victim's identity, I've taken the decision to issue a photograph to the press. With luck we should get a response pretty quickly. Dr Leadbetter's guess is she's one of the many foreign students who study here at one of the summer schools. Mike. Over to you."

Evans heaved his large frame from the sofa and, reaching for a clipboard, began to scribble on the white board, turning every so often to speak to them.

"OK. This is what we have so far. We now believe the two men in Bedminster were murdered and their bodies concealed behind the plasterboard approximately four years ago and certainly in the summer because of the evidence of insect remains found near the bodies. That takes us to June or July 1972. We've checked the electoral roll for the property. It was then owned by a Sikh landlord, a Mr Singh. Unfortunately he's since returned to the Punjab. Neither of the two men are listed as residents of the property so our guess is they were probably brought or lured here, then murdered. However, what we do have from the Missing Persons Bureau for the year in question are two names already known to us: Kevin Saunders and Michael Aswere. Both had form for cocaine dealing. Both lived in the same road in the St Paul's area. And, more importantly, both disappeared in the summer of 1972. Doug is checking dental records, so we should know pretty soon if we're right about them."

"OK," continued Glenister. "About our ice house victim. I had a phone call from Dave Thomas who, as you know, is presently working in Paris with the Sûreté. The woman's coat

57

was manufactured by a high-class company which operated in the Montmartre district. They supplied four haute couture shops in central Paris. The coat was part of a limited edition. Two of the shop outlets kept records of their customers' accounts and he's in the process of checking those against possible missing persons. Our other lines of enquiry have not yielded anything significant. Now, to the Brandon Hill murder. Doug, I believe you have something to add?"

"Not much detail on this as yet. We know that she was attacked at close range, probably by a carving knife. Her attacker was certainly no more than five feet six in height and because of her proximity to the victim; her clothing would certainly have been bloodstained. To what extent we don't know. We also have a very clear footprint of one of the trainers she was wearing. When we establish the identity of the victim we may be able to trace her whereabouts prior to the attack."

"Thanks Doug. Dr Leadbetter?"

"Just one observation really. There are two significant points which appear to provide a possible link between the Brandon Hill murder and the body in Woodfield Road. In both cases a type of duct tape was used to gag the victims. The fibres in each case are identical. Also, the Brandon Hill victim had a chunk of her hair cut off, indicating that the murderer had taken a trophy."

"You believe it's the same murderer?"

"I'm not at all definite about that. At present it's just one of a number of theories. If I'm right, however, it will mean we may have a problem. The fact that there's been a gap of a few years would indicate that something has happened, some key event in the murderer's life which has triggered this fresh attack. In which case we may expect a further attack at some time in the near future."

"Right, Frances. Thanks for that. Any questions then?"

There was a long silence during which Bottrell stifled a yawn.

"OK. For today, John, can you and Mike try and tie up the details about the Cotham residence. I'll be dealing with the press. I've scheduled a TV interview at 10am. Unless anything else breaks, we'll reconvene here tomorrow promptly at 9am."

* * *

When Bottrell made his way back to the flat, late that afternoon, he was ready to crash. The stifling heat of the city had become too much for him and as he made his way wearily up Whiteladies Road he kept thinking of his childhood days in West Cornwall and the salty tang of the sea air, which in summer would drive its way across the craggy, mine-pocked headland. He had spent sixteen precious years there with his parents, living in a small stone cottage on the edge of The Lizard. During the halcyon summer days of the holidays he would ride his bicycle down to a small bay on the coast, spending idyllic afternoons surfing or watching the dolphins and grey seals from the granite cliff top. When winter came and the tourists had packed up and gone, he would venture there still, at one with the wild winds and the white, seething spume of the Atlantic rollers as they crashed and boomed against the great cliffs.

He had never forgotten the feeling of space and remoteness in that far flung edge of the world. He wished he were there now and not slowly baking in this concrete, man-made oven that was the city. He crossed Clifton Park, drawing level with the grounds of Clifton College, its tall gothic spires glowing in the afternoon sunlight. On the cracked, dry earth a cricket match was in full swing, two batsmen running wearily up and down the line to the muted cheers of spectators.

"Mad dogs and Englishmen," he said to himself as he continued his way back to the flat, desperately seeking the shade of the trees as he did so. When he reached the flat and unlocked the door he found Anne Marie standing in the hallway, looking troubled.

"John," she said, "Could I speak to you please?"

*　*　*

She could not recall exactly when she had started to collect the dolls. The first had appeared in the refuse chute next to the bottom of the stairwell in the dingy block of flats in Redland. She often played alone here, waiting until the other children were out of the way, seeking solitude and darkness. She remembered the doll well for she had spotted its head peering up at her from a pile of rubbish. When she pulled at it, the head had detached itself and she was forced to climb into the trash to dig out the body. The doll's face had a wild, distracted look. One eye was missing and it had been badly scuffed. She had struck up an immediate empathy with the thing and had taken it back to the flat, concealed beneath her jacket. Having washed and bathed it, she had made underwear and a little skirt and top, cut out of scraps of material from her mother's sewing box, spending hours at night in her bedroom, hand sewing the pieces of material with infinite care.

When the work was complete, she had dressed the doll and placed it on her pillow, where she had sat and stared at it for a long while. That hot summer afternoon she realised something: that she had the power within her both to create and to destroy life. When the clothes had been fitted, the little figure had somehow come to life. She sewed an eye back into the socket and the doll looked back at her accusingly.

As time passed she acquired other dolls. Sometimes she would spot them on rubbish dumps and in people's dustbins, but it did not concern her that they had been discarded. What mattered most was that she had brought them in from the shadowland. She had given them shelter. She had given them life. And they were hers to do with as she wished.

In the end, there were seven of them in all, one for each day of the week, kept in a battered suitcase beneath her bed. At night, when her mother was sleeping, she would open the case and lay them out on her bed. When the moon shone through her bedroom window, she would turn them to face its ghostly rays and their faces would come alive in the shadows of the room and they would whisper to her then in scarcely audible voices, telling her their secrets and misfortunes.

Then, one day in winter, when she was thirteen, her mother found the suitcase. She had returned home late after a swimming lesson and found her mother standing at the door to her bedroom, that smile upon her face she had grown to hate and fear, a smile of malice and cunning. She stood with her arms folded, accusing her of keeping secrets from her, her voice strident and harsh, her eyes blazing with a manic fury.

After this the dolls were consigned to the dustbin and she to her room, bearing the marks of her punishment. It was then that she had developed the ideas of atonement and sacrifice. It was a simple theory, crudely formed but for one so young, it was an amazingly adult notion. She came to believe that for each act of cruelty or unkindness there must be an equivalent act. Action and reaction, was this not the law of the universe. So she had been taught. That each action she took had a repercussion. When she was bullied at school she sought out some small, helpless creature and tortured it. Insects and small mammals were her prey. For her suffering to be alleviated, she must cause others to suffer.

She knelt down and picked up the doll to examine it. It was one of those large Victorian dolls with dark, mournful eyes, the hair long and dark, the skin a cream-coloured porcelain. It was prettily clothed in a long, paisley dress with blue knickerbockers and high heeled boots. She had spotted it from the other side of the park, lying on the edge of the path. It had probably slipped out of a pram or been dropped by some careless child. She looked around but there was no one about. She stroked its hair, whispering to it. The eyes looked back at her, deep wells of sorrow. She would take it to her room of quickening, restore it to life and it would give her succour and guidance.

It was the day after that she had decided to act. Each day that she went into the room the voices seemed louder and more insistent until at last she could stand their babble no more. They cried out for atonement. In the morning she had bathed and prepared herself, donning the coat and wig and sunglasses. Then she had walked down into the city and sat and listened, knowing that her chance would come if she stayed here long enough. And, after what seemed an eternity of waiting, that moment arrived.

That same afternoon she had cleaned the knife and placed it back in the rack. She had burned the coat in the hearth, relieved that she had been able to slip back to the house unseen. No one had seen the blood. She smiled in remembrance and bagged up the ashes. Then she had returned to the quickening room. The voices were hushed now, full of quiet contemplation. And the doll with the sorrowful eyes stared back at her but made no comment on what she had done, for truly there was nothing to be said.

* * *

Anne Marie had stayed for about an hour. Bottrell had been so exhausted when he had arrived back at the flat that he had groaned inwardly on seeing her but there was something about the young Frenchwoman which made him reconsider his inhospitable feelings towards her. Over fresh coffee she began to unburden herself. Since moving into the flat in September she had been troubled.

"Troubled? By what?"

"By noises."

"How do you mean?"

"Noises. I hear them at night, in the room next to mine."

"What sort of noises?"

"The sound of a woman's voice. First she is weeping, then crying out."

"Have you spoken to your neighbour in the flat beneath you?"

"No, no. It is not from the flat downstairs. I have asked. The voice is from the room itself. I know it is strange. Have you also heard this?"

Bottrell thought about the figure he had seen in the garden but decided not to mention it.

"No. I haven't heard anything."

"At first I thought I had imagined it. But it has happened so many times now. And there is a smell also, which comes when the voice is there."

"What sort of smell?"

"A smell of roses, I think. It is difficult for me to describe. And when I hear this voice there is a terrible feeling of... triste.

63

How do you say? Sadness. Do you think that maybe the flat has a ghost?"

"I don't know. Look, would you be willing to show me the room?"

They finished their coffee and made their way across the landing. The small hallway smelled of garlic, and the afternoon light shone in through an open window, picking out the golds and reds of the heavy curtains.

Anne Marie turned and opened the door to the second bedroom. He looked inside, hovering at the threshold for a moment, trying to suspend all thought, allowing the presence of the room to filter into his consciousness. The room had been brightly decorated in a soft buttermilk and was equipped with a comfortable, contemporary style bed with a patchwork quilt. Apart from a small Edwardian wardrobe, a pine bedside table, lamp and a bookcase, there appeared to be nothing remarkable or out of place here.

Yet something in the room made him stiffen. He had experienced something like this years before when his mother had taken him to a neighbour's house in Bristol. There was one room in the building which he had found intensely cold and which he had always been loath to enter. It was only in later years that he discovered one of its previous residents had committed suicide there.

But what was it about this room? It was nothing overt or tangible, yet he continued to hover on the threshold, reluctant to enter. He became conscious of Anne Marie staring at him, no doubt wondering why he said nothing.

"What is it?" she said at last, forcing the moment. "What do you feel here?"

"I'm not sure," he replied. But I think you're right. There's something not quite right about the room."

Afterwards, when he had returned to his flat, he poured himself a whisky and sat, trying to blot out the memory of the room. Although he had said nothing more to Anne Marie for fear of alarming her, he had been deeply troubled. He rarely told others about his 'gift' as he termed it but it was something he had come to rely on over the years. It was his sixth sense, an ability to read people and places and see what others did not. His mother had had it too. Hence her deep interest in spiritualism. Sometimes it was a curse, telling him things he had rather not know, burdening him with past memories and events.

One thing was clear. Anne Marie had been right about the flat. There was something in this building, some melancholy event which had seeped into its fabric. Why had his mother not mentioned it to him? It was curious. Surely she would have sensed it?

He finished his whisky and stood by the window, looking out across the garden. The sun was low on the horizon now, long shadows engulfing the city. A heat haze had risen, refracting the light, giving an orange glow to the edge of the tall buildings. Far off, in the east, the moon had risen, its horns sharp-edged against the deep blue of the night sky.

He reached for the bottle and refilled his glass. Then, switching on the small table lamp, he sank into the chair, listening to the distant sounds of the city.

CHAPTER FIVE
MEMORIES

The morning briefing at No 27 Great George St was kept short. Glenister, who was more irascible than usual this morning, informed the team that there had been a development. Since the article had appeared in the *Bristol Evening Post* and his appeal on HTV, he had been contacted by a Language School in Pembroke Road, informing him that a French student, one Rachael La Mer, had been reported missing from her lodgings in Redland. It was a hopeful lead.

The air in the office was now almost unbearable. So hot in fact that Bottrell and Evans had opted for iced water instead of their usual coffee. Since their last encounter, Evans had been busy checking the CRO records. It appeared that Kevin Saunders had been living with his girlfriend in a squat in Brownton Road, Bedminster, prior to his disappearance in the summer of 1972 and since she had also been charged with possession, her name was still on record.

Thanet Road was a cul-de-sac not far from Parson Street Railway Station. Number 15 lay in the middle of the terrace, a drab, unexceptional council building from the mid 60s, its front garden cluttered with pieces of car engine, a broken children's climbing frame, several chunks of metal and a wrecked moped. Evans and Bottrell parked the car at the end of the road and made their way to the front door, conscious of the watchful gaze of a small gang of youngsters. Bottrell hoped the car would be safe.

Since there was no doorbell Evans rapped hard on the peeling, brown door. He waited for a while, then shouted through the letterbox. There was another long pause, the sound of the door chain being removed, then finally the door opened, revealing a tall, large-framed man with dreadlocks. A waft of stale food and cannabis smoke drifted out to meet the two detectives.

"Police. Could we have a word?" asked Evans, showing his warrant card.

"What's this about, man?" came the reply.

Behind the man Bottrell glimpsed a short, thin-faced woman holding a baby in her arms, which she appeared to be breastfeeding. She quickly disappeared from view.

"We'd like to speak to Michelle Brown. She lives here I believe?"

"What's this all about?" the tall man repeated, this time more aggressively.

"It's OK. It's only a routine enquiry. Nothing else."

"We just need to have a word with her, that's all. Can we speak to her?" Bottrell said.

The woman reappeared, readjusted her clothing, lowered the baby into a carrycot, then moved forward to face Bottrell.

"It's OK, Ashley," she said. "I'll talk to them."

The big man shrugged his shoulders.

"I'll be in the kitchen if you need help," he said, eyeing the men warily.

"Is this about Kevin?" she asked, sitting down at a table by the window, where the morning light threw her face into relief. Although she could only have been in her late-twenties, her face had been ravaged by time, her complexion pitted and mottled, while her eyes bore the familiar signs of drug abuse. Bottrell, who remained standing, let Evans do the talking while his eyes scanned the room. Piles of old newspapers were stashed all around the room. On a low coffee table stood a large glass ashtray, stacked full of dog ends. Bottrell wondered if they should investigate the contents. He knew, from the smell, what they would find, but that wasn't why they were here. That could wait. There was a stale, greasy smell in the house as if someone had just finished cooking. He felt sorry for the baby.

"I understand that you were Kevin Saunder's girlfriend. This would have been about four years ago when you were living in the Bedminster area?"

"I was one of his women – yes."

"And did you work for him in Bedminster?"

Michelle stifled a yawn and, opening a fresh packet of cigarettes, lit one, sucking down the acrid smoke. She coughed a deep, shuddering, bronchial cough which rippled in waves from her worn lungs.

"Yes, there were three of us. We did work for him in a massage parlour in Bartlett Road."

"He was your pimp?" Evans asked bluntly.

"Listen. I don't have to sit here and take this from some white trash copper! Understand? We just worked for him, that's all I'm saying."

Evans moved back in the chair, trying to avoid the fumes from her cigarette.

"You knew he had a record for dealing, of course?"

"Kevin was called the sweetie man. You name it, he could get it for you. He had half the kids in the area working for him. I didn't like that. Fancy using kids! I've done some stuff in my time but I wouldn't stoop that low."

"Were they his couriers?"

She nodded, bleakly.

"And when did you last see him?"

She thought for a moment, trying to trawl up the memories from a dark place.

"Summer of 1972, I think. He'd been cutting some good quality heroin and had a distribution thing going at the back of the parlour. It had a side door where customers could come and go without any bother."

"Were you aware that he had enemies?"

"Rivals – of course. Goes with the territory. You want me to name names? I can't do that. That's too risky."

"What about his friend?"

"Michael? Yeah I knew him too."

"Do you know anyone still around in the area we could speak to who might have harboured a grudge against him?"

She finished her cigarette, then added it to the graveyard of cigarette butts.

"Try the massage parlour on Waterloo Road. Ask for Roy N'como. But don't mention my name."

* * *

Jean-Paul had been missing Rachael. He had spent twenty minutes waiting outside the library on Whiteladies Road. It was unlike her not to turn up. A tall, gangly boy of seventeen, he and Rachael were lifelong friends. In fact he had known her since the age of nine when they had both attended the same school in the Rue de Picard. Like Rachael, his father was wealthy and keen to encourage his son's proficiency in English. So it was that they had been found host families in Bristol, not far from the Language School in Pembroke Road.

He looked at his watch. 9.10am. He would be late for his first session now. Giving a final glance up and down the road, he decided to head off.

Ronald Savageri, the head of the Belmont Language School, had also been delayed that morning. On leaving the house in Redland Road, he had discovered that one of his tyres had been slashed, which seemed to him to be an act of incomprehensible vandalism. He had cursed loudly and began to walk through the sweltering streets to the school. How could it be so hot this early? He really would have to try and lose some weight.

When he arrived, drenched in sweat, he headed straight for the cooled water machine near the entrance and drank the iced cold water gratefully. The clipped tones of Sally Acre, his receptionist, distracted him.

"I had Mr and Mrs Wickham on the phone this morning, Ronald. It seems that Rachael La Mer failed to return to her lodgings last night."

Savageri lumbered over to the hatch, where he stood like some beached whale, dabbing at his forehead with a soiled handkerchief.

"And they haven't seen her since?"

"No." Sally stared back at him. "Are you feeling OK?"

"Quite alright, thank you Sally. And if you're wondering why I'm late, my car was vandalised last night."

"Do you think we should phone the police about Rachael?" Sally asked. "Only I happened to read the *Bristol Evening Post* last night and there was a description in it of a girl they found on Brandon Hill. I thought it looked a bit like – well, it wasn't much of a description of course, but I just thought it might be her."

"I'll phone them Sally. Just give me a moment, will you? You didn't happen to keep the paper, did you?"

70

"No, it's at home."

Adjusting his tie, Savageri disappeared into his office.

* * *

The massage parlour in Waterloo Road came as no surprise to Bottrell and Evans. It ran parallel with Old Market, just up from the harbour, a wide road with tall, late-Victorian villas which had seen better days. Bottrell had parked the car in West Street, where he and Evans had spotted a greasy spoon cafe. Bottrell sighed wearily. It would be hot, humid and greasy in there but Evans was adamant. By the time they left, some twenty minutes later, both men's clothes were impregnated with the smells of a hundred fry-ups.

Back on the street, Bottrell wound down the car window, then switched on the radio. He had a brief conversation while Evans waited for him on the corner of the street.

"Anything useful?" he asked when Bottrell had finished.

"It seems Mr N'como has no shortage of form. GBH, and procuring. Spent some time in Horfield prison for burglary."

"A regular nice guy then."

By now they were almost level with the door of the Swingers Massage Parlour. Evans pressed the intercom button. Immediately a voice answered.

"Let us in please. Police. We need to see Mr N'como."

The intercom buzzed and the door opened. They found themselves in a small, windowless reception area where the only lighting was a tall, old fashioned standard lamp and a hideous looking aluminium spotlight. Behind a desk in the centre of the room stood a well-built black girl. She was dressed in a low, close fitting white top and her long legs were barely concealed by a short black leather miniskirt.

"You want Mr N'como?" she asked, avoiding eye contact with both men.

"That's correct," replied Evans.

"He's not available. Not without an appointment."

"We don't need an appointment. Kindly inform him we need to see him. Otherwise I'm sure we can find him ourselves."

Evans moved towards the desk. The girl glanced at him sullenly, then disappeared through a baize curtain. Bottrell and Evans sat down opposite a client, obviously a businessman. But he took one look at them and moved quickly from the house. Evans laughed.

"Oops! Looks like we've spoilt their trade!"

He was still laughing when the girl returned. She looked very annoyed when she saw the man had gone.

"Mr N'como will see you. Through here please."

They passed through the curtain into a narrow hallway with a series of rooms leading off. They could hear the faint sounds of appreciative customers. Evans grinned at Bottrell. At the end of the corridor was a door marked 'Strictly Private'. She stopped and knocked twice. The door opened. A tall, powerfully built man in his early thirties stood in the doorway. The heat was oppressive and his sleeves were rolled up, showing off his muscular arms. He had large, deep eyes, a broken nose and on his left ear hung a silver pendant. He smelled of aftershave – a hint of musk, Bottrell thought.

"Mr N'como?"

"Come in gentlemen. Sit down. I'm always ready to help the police. Take no notice of the girl. Now. How may I help you?"

The voice was clipped and self-assured.

"I understand you knew Michael Aswere."

The big man blinked slowly, then stared at Bottrell.

72

"Sure I did. Strictly past tense."

"Meaning?"

"Meaning I haven't seen him for a long, long time."

"You knew he'd disappeared then?"

"I was aware of it, yes."

Bottrell had noticed a small tattoo on his left forearm, depicting a skull and crossbones with the initials 'SCB'.

"What was the exact nature of your relationship with Michael?" asked Evans.

N'como steepled his hands, his finely manicured nails meeting.

"Michael and me, we go back a long way. To Kingston, Jamaica. Brothers. Part of the same tribe. But that all changed when we came here. We tried for a while to fight for the black cause. I opened a bookshop on Old Market. We used it as our campaign headquarters. Then he changed. Met up with this other guy."

"Kevin Saunders?"

He nodded.

"Precisely so. Until that point Michael had been clean. Relatively speakin'. I mean it's a matter of degree. That's what I'm sayin' to you. We all smoke the ganja. That's part of our religion, you understand. But I never touched no hard drugs. Know what I'm sayin'. This Saunders guy was into it big time. Cocaine, heroin, LSD, you name it, he supplied it. In two years he had supplied half of Bedminster. Children as young as ten hooked on the stuff. And they were using young kids as runners for the stuff. But that's not all."

"What else?"

"They were into guns in a big way. Getting them from Jamaica through Bristol Airport. Not just hand guns either. Semi-automatics. They'd break them down into parts and bring them in that way. I told Michael he was storing up trouble for himself. He had the lifestyle alright. The expensive suits, the jewellery, the Mercedes. But he had enemies too. He and Saunders were working a protection racket at some of the clubs in the St Paul's area. Once there was an incident. A guy was shot. It was soon after that I lost touch with him. I assumed he'd gone back to Jamaica until the heat had died down. So – he's resurfaced again?"

"He's dead," Bottrell replied. "He and Saunders were found a day ago in a house in Bedminster Parade."

There was a pause. Bottrell thought N'como looked genuinely surprised at the news. Just then the door opened and the leggy receptionist entered.

"Sorry to interrupt, Roy, but there's a punter in cubicle six says he hasn't any cash for his – massage." She paused then continued. "Will we take American Express?"

N'como's face registered mild amusement.

"Leave it to me," he said, rising to his full six feet. "Gentlemen, you'll have to wait or come back later. Business."

* * *

Ronald Savageri stared long and hard at the photograph, before easing his immense girth back into the office chair.

"Well?" asked Glenister. "Is it her, do you think?"

"I'm not absolutely certain, though, at first glance, I must say it looks rather like Rachael. The problem is, Inspector, and I'll be frank with you, if I may – the thing is, as a language school, we have a great number of foreign students passing through our doors in the summer months. As you might imagine, most of them are here for a short duration. So many faces, it's difficult to recall each one, if you get my drift."

Glenister nodded. He'd got the drift.

"But you say Rachael La Mer is missing from classes today?"

"Yes, as I told someone on the phone, she didn't return home last night to her host parents."

"They phoned the school?"

"Well no, it was her friend, Helene Pickard, who informed our receptionist. I phoned Mr and Mrs Wickham, the host parents, and they confirmed the story. Obviously they're very concerned."

"Where exactly was she lodging?"

"Alexandra Road. Sally, my receptionist, will give you the address if you like."

"This Helene ..."

"Helene Pickard."

"I'd like to speak to her. How is her English?"

"Very good."

Savageri leaned forward and pressed the intercom.

"Sally. See if you can get hold of Helene Pickard for me, will you? I'd like a word with her. She should be in – let me see – Norman Stanton's class, Room 6."

There was a silence as Savageri eased himself back into the chair and seemed at a loss for something to say. Glenister sat listening to the sounds of the students' voices as they ebbed and flowed in the corridor outside and wished he had a cigarette. Before long there was a timid knock at the door.

"Come!" commanded the principal.

The door opened. A young man with gold-rimmed glasses and dark curly hair hovered on the threshold. Next to him stood a short, round-faced girl with straight, black hair pulled back into a ponytail.

"Mademoiselle Acre told us to come up and see you, sir," said the girl, in a strong French accent.

"Yes, that's right, Helene. Come in, both of you and sit down. This is Chief Inspector Glenister. He wants to ask you some questions about Rachael La Mer."

The two sat down and looked apprehensively in Glenister's direction.

"Don't worry," Savageri assured them. "You're not in any trouble. Why exactly are you here, Jean-Paul?"

"I met Helene at class this morning. She told me about Rachael."

"You are Rachael's boyfriend?" Glenister asked.

The boy nodded.

"We are friends, yes. I have known her since very small, since I was with her in Normandy."

"And you are also a friend of Rachael's?"

The young girl blushed.

"You lodge together?"

"We are friends, yes."

"And Rachael was missing this morning?"

"She didn't come home with us last night."

"Exactly where were you last night?"

"A group of us, we went to the riverside."

"Where exactly on the riverside?"

"At the pub. The old pub on the river."

"The Llandogger Trow? Was that the name of the pub?"

She nodded.

"Yes. I do not know how to say the name."

"And she was with you all the time?"

"Yes. She stayed with us all the evening."

"And what time did you leave?"

"About eleven, I think. Yes, it must have been eleven."

"And Rachael left with you?"

"Yes, although I did not notice her very much, I was talking to Jean-Paul." She blushed again.

Glenister turned to Jean-Paul.

"You weren't with Rachael at the pub?"

"No."

"Why not?"

"We had had a falling out. Just a silly row."

"What was it about?" pressed Glenister.

"I think she thought I did not spend time with her. That I was more interested in Helene." The boy looked mortified. "It was not true. Just a silly row..."

"So you didn't speak to her all the while you were at the pub?"

"I spoke to her, yes – when we first met at the pub. But only for a few moments. She was not in a good mood with me. I feel very bad about this."

"And you didn't meet up with her afterwards?"

"No. I didn't see where she went after the pub. I thought she was with some of the girls."

"What sort of girl was Rachael? Was she a shy girl or was she friendly and outward going?"

"She was quite shy," Helene answered. She was very subdued.

"So, apart from you and Jean-Paul, did she ever meet anyone else?"

They both shook their heads.

"OK. That's as much as I need."

"Alright, Helene, Jean-Paul. You can return to classes." said Savageri, thoughtfully.

"What about Rachael? Is it true that she has been murdered?" Helene asked. "Is it true what they have been saying?"

"I can't say for certain yet."

Savageri stood up and moved towards the door.

"Back to class now, you two. Come and see me this afternoon. We'll talk then."

When they had gone, he turned to Glenister. "You believe the girl to be Rachael?"

"I'm pretty certain of it, yes. We need to be certain. For now, we need to keep this under wraps. I'd appreciate your co-operation in the matter. Please don't talk to the press."

"Certainly. You have my word. You'll let me know?"

"As soon as we're sure, of course."

Glenister stood up, ready to leave. The room was stifling and airless and the smell of sweat coming from Savageri was too much.

"I'll be in touch, Mr Savageri."

As Glenister made his way down the brightly lit corridor, a short, podgy man in a torn tweed jacket pushed past him. Glenister turned to stare at him as the overpowering smell of eau de cologne filled the air. He thought the man seemed agitated and ill at ease.

"Mr Stanton," he heard Savageri say, "you look upset. What's wrong?"

Then he disappeared from view, shutting the principal's door behind him.

* * *

The two bodies lay side by side on the mortuary tables. To Bottrell they resembled those Egyptian mummies which had so

78

fascinated him as a child when his mother had taken him to the Bristol Museum. There, in the half-lit corridor, he had stared in awful fascination at the yellowed, parchment skin behind their glass cases.

Walker leaned over the bodies in his white lab coat like some strange vulture, and adjusted the spotlight, training it on the arms of the deceased.

Bottrell stared at the hazy, blurred outline of the tattoo as Walker sank the blade of his scalpel into the surface of the desiccated skin, moving it slowly back until he had etched a rectangle with it, then peeling the section of the skin away with his fingers.

"Quite indistinct isn't it?" he said as he slipped the skin fragment into a bag.

"Probably quite old by the time the victim died."

"And what are you going to do with it? asked Bottrell.

"Put it in a 3 per cent solution of hydrogen peroxide and let it marinade for a wee bit. Then it should be a lot clearer."

Moving to the side of the room he took the flap of skin from the bag and with a pair of forceps plunged it into a beaker of liquid. They waited. Beyond the room, in the streets below, Bottrell could hear the wail of a police siren.

"You say this N'como character had a tattoo?"

"Yes, on his forearm. A skull and crossbones and some letters."

Walker nodded and, turning to the beaker, lifted the piece of skin clear of the solution, then lay it on the table and began drying it with a piece of tissue.

"Something like this?" he asked.

Bottrell stared.

"Exactly like this," he replied.

SCB. What did they stand for, he wondered. Some sort of society maybe?

CHAPTER SIX
FRENCH CONNECTION

She had not always been like this. There had been a time when things had been very different, when she was very young and the world had not seemed such a threatening place. In those early years in Redland, her mother had been relatively happy and the demon that slept inside her had still not surfaced. The new man who came to their house in those early years was tall and dark with smiling eyes. He had a way with children and it was clear, even to her young mind, that her mother was deeply in love with this man whom she called Jack. In those days, they lived in a ground floor flat which consisted of two large Victorian bedrooms, a sitting room, a small kitchen and bathroom. The sitting room had tall French windows which opened out onto an overgrown garden. At the end of the garden was a small stream where she would spend hours floating paper boats or watching the small, gossamer-winged damselflies. In summer, the long grass was full of delicate wild orchids and in the autumn the ancient oaks and elders were covered with orange fungi. It was her magical and enchanted place, where she could lie in the long grass and listen to the songs of countless birds and the rustle of insects.

But it didn't last. One day she returned to the house and found her mother weeping in the kitchen. There were bruises on her face and there was blood on her hands. An empty bottle of wine on the kitchen table and her mother's slurred speech told her the rest. She asked where Jack was but her mother did not reply. She retreated into silence and did not speak to her until the following morning.

Jack never returned and when autumn came, they left the flat and moved to the house on the Woodstock Road, leaving behind her place of magic where the quickened spirits came and went in the old garden. And with that move, her power left her. The support and company of the voices had deserted her. She was truly alone.

Her mother changed too, and not for the better. She continued to drink heavily, not just wine but spirits too. In the evening she would often be drunk but also in the mornings. And with her drunkenness came the violence.

The new house in Woodstock Road was not like the old place. A tall, glowering, red brick villa, it stood in a road facing other red brick villas. There was nothing of character about it. The rooms were large and cheerless and the heating, a collection of antiquated storage heaters, was woefully inadequate.

The sitting room and her bedroom faced east and when winter came she and her mother froze as the easterly wind found its way through the cracks in the dilapidated window frames. By now, her mother had lost her lucrative job and was living on benefits and the remains of her meagre savings. They ate infrequently, usually chips with whatever they could find in the cupboard, and when her mother was drunk they often did not eat at all. Then, at the age of twelve, the bad dream became a nightmare. Her mother sent her to the local comprehensive.

The school had been named after a wealthy merchant venturer and philanthropist, a man who had made millions from the slave trade. However, the school lay far from the magic of

Bristol's dreaming spires. Built in the early 1960s, its bold and functional architecture bestowed on its staff and pupils a depressing sense of despair. Within twelve years its substandard classrooms and dim corridors bore a war-weary look. Staff came and went at the school like commuters on a busy railway terminus and the Head of this 1,200-strong community wore a permanently fazed expression as if he were suffering from shell shock. On an average day at least half of the permanent staff were off sick, the numbers being made up by supply teachers who rarely lasted more than a day. At break times the toilets were opened but during lessons they were locked by the caretakers to prevent widespread vandalism.

There were places on the site where duty staff rarely ventured for reasons of personal security and there were often assaults on both children and staff in the school's dark corridors.

She arrived at the school on a grey day in early autumn. From the outset, she knew instinctively that she would be a target. For a start, she was shorter than average for her twelve years. Due to her poor diet she was much too overweight. Her flesh was pale and stretched and her eyes bore a permanently worried look. On that first day she stood on the edge of the playground, wishing that she were anywhere but here. Her fears were soon to be confirmed.

On her second day, as she made her way down the narrow corridor that led to 'B' block, she was confronted by a group of older girls who surrounded her and demanded money and sweets. When she explained she had neither, she was beaten and spat on.

As the weeks passed, the pattern repeated itself. She came to dread and loathe the break and lunch times. She developed the strategy of hiding in the school library or merging herself in amongst large groups of pupils so that she would not be noticed. But she could not keep this up forever.

It was in the library that she found her escape from the brutalities of the school's tribalism. The volumes its shelves contained offered her a door into another world. Within a year she had worked her way through the more popular juvenile authors and by the second year she had begun reading Dickens, Wells and Austen. Between the pages of these books she saw once more the quickening of the human spirit. She read about love, suffering, poverty and death. She loved these secret worlds where the author acted as God, pulling the strings of his puppet creations. She knew then that if she had been given sufficient talent she too could have become a writer, shaping her secret worlds in her own image. These books were her sustenance. Wherever she went she would carry one with her. Even in class she would be sitting reading, a book wedged between her legs and the desk, half of her mind listening to the drone of the teacher's voice, the other half adrift in some imaginary world of adventure. In that far away world she rode with horses, flew with angels and fought with heroes.

But there was always that other reality, that world of petty spitefulness, intrigue and cruelty which formed the main agenda of her day at the comprehensive. The two girls who bullied her the most were Sandra Hayes and Hazel Blicken. Sandra Hayes was a tall, overweight girl in the fourth year who ran a protection racket among the younger girls. Six feet tall, with blonde hair scraped back into a severe ponytail, she could be spotted immediately at the far end of the corridor. There was something which repulsed her on their first encounter. Sandra could spot a victim a mile off. She had a nose for it. Even on her first day at school Sandra had pinned her up against a wall, stripping her of her meagre possessions. She and Hazel were a team. Even their names induced a spasm of fear in young hearts. For the first two terms they conducted a reign of terror against her. It culminated in the toilet incident at the end of the Easter term.

She had decided that she had had enough. On that particular morning she had walked to school, reasoning with herself that she could no longer go on being a victim. So, at breakfast, when Hazel and Sandra stopped her in the B block corridor to ask for money, she had refused. Her nightmare began at lunchtime. She was about to leave the girls' toilets when the door suddenly opened, revealing the two of them.

"Time to pay, dogpiss!" said Sandra.

Hazel slipped behind her and pinned her arms behind her back. Then they dragged her into a cubicle, inverted her and lowered her into the lavatory bowl, pulling the chain. The cold, fetid water gushed into her mouth and nostrils, choking her. They repeated the exercise four times, all the while abusing her, until at last she staggered from the cubicle, her head and blouse soaked, coughing and spluttering.

"Next time," said Sandra, grinning, "make sure you remember when it's pay day."

The memory of that ordeal remained with her throughout the Easter holidays. During that two and a half weeks she thought long and hard about how she would take her revenge. In the end she followed a simple plan.

On the second day of the summer term she stood among a large crowd of pupils in the narrow corridor between A and B block. She had noted this place before. Long and poorly lit, it offered the perfect opportunity for an unseen attack.

At morning break time four classes converged on this spot and it was further swamped by members of the upper school attempting to gain access to the art and sports blocks. The nearest member of staff was two corridors away.

She stood outside the door to Room 9, hidden by a gaggle of second year girls who were pushing and shoving each other. She knew Sandra would appear in the corridor because she had plotted her movements.

In the pocket of her blazer was a long scalpel with a sharp, pointed blade. She had spent the previous evening gently stroking the blade and murmuring incantations under her breath. It was razor sharp. Thoughts of revenge flooded through her. She could feel the power returning. She had cut a small hole into the side of her pocket so that the blade could be driven through it in one single blow.

Before long she could hear the loud Bristolean tones of Sandra Hayes, her blonde head six inches above the heads of the other girls. She drew level with her but so deep in conversation was she that she didn't see her. Suddenly she spotted a gap in the crowd. She stepped forward and with a single thrust, drove the blade into the small of Sandra's back. The razor edge cut through the cloth of her jacket as if it were butter, then entered the flesh to the left of her spine. She heard the big girl cry out with pain. She stumbled, her hands flailing, then she was down on the ground, gurgling blood. She realised, in that moment of elation, that she must have punctured one of her lungs.

One of the girls started screaming and a small crowd gathered round the writhing figure. But by now she had moved out into the quadrangle and was heading for the security of the library with a very large smile on her face.

* * *

DC Dave Thomas finished his cappuccino, stubbed out his Camel cigarette, then waved at the *garçon*. The young waiter with the sleek black hair approached the table.

"Six francs," he said, his face a mask of indifference. Not wishing to embarrass himself by attempting a reply in French, Thomas said nothing but rummaged in his jacket pocket, then pulled out a ten franc note and handed it to him. The waiter disappeared for a moment, then returned with a plate bearing four coins. Thomas took three and left the remainder as a tip. He wasn't sure it would be enough. One thing he was sure of though, after a week of unrewarding investigation, he was now within a whisker of discovering the identity of the ice house victim.

The mac worn by the murdered woman had been sold in only four high quality clothes shops in central Paris. All four of them had kept detailed records of their wealthy customer's transactions. Moreover, the macs were part of a limited edition, each one carrying a unique number. On the inside of the seam was printed the number 37520. Unfortunately, two of the fashion shops did not match the specific numbers with individual customers. The third did so but 37520 was not listed.

It was now going to be a matter of luck with shop number four. 'Joie de Vivre' stood in the Rue du Croissant, near to the Bourse des Valeurs. Since the day was unbearably hot, he decided to leave the Metro and, using his large scale map of the city, walked north east through a series of narrow streets. The city was alive at this hour and congested with heavy traffic. He crossed the Rue Montmartre, narrowly escaping a collision with a 2CV, then took a left turn into the Place des Victoires, where he consulted a newsvendor about his intended destination. Fortunately for Thomas, the man spoke good English. 'Joie de Vivre' was further up the street, an elegant art deco building whose tall windows sported a series of female dummies dressed in the height of French fashion.

'Le Patron' in fact, turned out to be a tall, sleek woman in her mid-forties, dressed in an exquisitely-made suit. Speaking perfect English, she invited him into a room at the back of the premises, lined with mahogany panelling and furnished with brass-studded leather easy chairs.

"Monsieur Colbert of the Sûreté told us you needed our help," she began.

"Yes, we're trying to trace the owner of one of your garments. A belted mac." He produced a photograph from his jacket pocket and placed it on the table in front of her.

"Exactly so. One of our Saint Marie range. A limited edition. We no longer supply this item."

"Do you happen to keep a record of who you sold them to?"

"One moment please."

She disappeared into a side room and re-emerged bearing a large black ring binder. "*Voilà*. Our records show we sold twenty of these items between 1970 and 1972."

"Did you happen to record the unique number of each coat?"

"I do," she replied. He gave her the number.

"Let me see. Ah yes, here it is. A Mme Isabelle Le Conte."

"Do you have an address?"

"Apt 26, No 25, Rue Huysmans."

"Where is that exactly?"

"It's in the southern part of the city."

"Thank you. You've been most helpful."

Rue Huysmans was over two miles away, south of the Seine. His cab wound its way slowly through endless traffic, the air full of the blazing horns of frustrated drivers. They crossed the Seine, the old river shimmering in the afternoon heat. The cab driver talked to him endlessly about English football but Thomas, a rugby man, had little to say on the matter.

Number 25 was one of a series of tall, yellow-brick villas, thrown up at the end of the nineteenth century to accommodate the *nouveau riche* of Paris. One hundred years later the yellow brick had turned black with coal soot and the large window frames were peeling and worn. Apt 26 was on the fourth floor, contacted by an outmoded brass intercom. Thomas pressed the button and waited. There was a slight pause, then a man's voice answered.

"Oui."

"Monsieur Le Conte?"

"Oui."

"I am a police officer from England. Could I speak to you please?"

The door buzzed, then opened admitting him into a dark hallway, painted in a heavy brown varnish. Two doors lay to his left while to his right was an old fashioned lift with a concertina door. He stepped inside, closed the door and pressed the button for "23 - 26". The lift creaked upwards, then juddered to a halt at floor 4. Through the gap in the lift door he could see the outline of an elderly woman in a fur coat. A small Pekinese dog yapped at her ankles. She stared at him suspiciously before disappearing quickly into her apartment.

As he slid back the lift door, the flat door opposite opened. A short, grey-haired man stood in the doorway, puffing away at a short, briar pipe.

"Monsieur Le Conte?" Thomas asked.

The man extended a thin hand in greeting.

"Jean Le Conte. What's this all about?"

Over cognacs, Jean Le Conte gave an account of his wife's disappearance. They had first visited Britain with their small daughter in the summer of 1970 when he had been employed at Bristol University as part of an exchange lectureship. Le Conte, who spoke fluent English, explained how his wife Isabelle had met a painter at one of the university's social gatherings.

"What was his name?" asked Thomas.

"Jack Slade. He was an abstract painter. Lectured part time at the university's art school campus. Isabelle had formed an instant attachment to him."

"They had an affair?"

"Not at first, no. Not in the physical sense. When we returned to France she corresponded with him regularly. She refused to show me his letters. It caused much trouble between us. This is very difficult for me, you understand. After that we gradually drifted apart. Then, in the summer of 1972, she just disappeared."

"Did she leave you a note?"

"No note. Nothing. I woke up one morning and she had gone."

"You never heard from her after that?"

Le Conte shook his head.

"I was very hurt that she should do this. Of course, I made enquiries. I wrote to the university about this man Slade but they would not give me his details. I assumed that they were living together in his flat. But I could never confirm it. I persisted for a while like this, then I just gave up. It was what she wanted, I thought. So – where is she then?"

Thomas coughed awkwardly. Informing the relatives of the deceased was something he hated.

"We think we've found your wife," he said, slowly measuring his words, trying not to meet Le Conte's gaze.

"We believe she may have been murdered."

For a moment Le Conte stared at him in disbelief.

"Murdered?" he exclaimed. "What do you mean?"

"Her body was discovered a few weeks ago, in an ice house in the garden of a house in the Redland area. We believe she was murdered about four years ago. We were only able to identify her because she was wearing a distinctive white coat."

Thomas produced the photograph of the raincoat.

"Do you recognise this as belonging to your wife?"

Le Conte nodded, tears welling up.

"*Mon Dieu*! How could this happen? Yes – I think it is hers. I'm certain. She had such style. How… how did she die?"

"I'm sorry, Monsieur. She was stabbed."

"Stabbed? Who would do that? Why did no one find her body earlier? All this time I thought… thought she was with him."

Le Conte's voice broke.

"All those years in that place."

"Her body had been well concealed and the garden where she was found, was very overgrown. It happens like that sometimes…"

"And her murderer?"

"We have few leads at present I'm afraid. Her attacker was careful to hide the evidence. Now that we know who she was, things should be a little easier. This painter —"

"Jack Slade?"

"I don't suppose you have his address?"

"No, as I told you. The university refused to disclose this. What – do you think he was involved?"

"I've no idea at this stage. Was there anyone else she knew in Bristol? Anyone you can think of that she might have met when you were staying there?"

"Apart from the faculty staff, no, I can't think of anyone in particular. We spent most of our time together – apart from when she met Slade. She was a beautiful woman of course…"

His voice petered out. Thomas felt for him.

"What sort of person was this Slade character?"

"I only met him a couple of times. He was handsome I suppose. Older than Isabelle. I think that was part of the attraction. He had – how shall I say – charisma? Yes. charisma. Even I could see that. A ladies' man. When she met him we had been married for twelve years. Things had become passionless."

"So it didn't come as a complete surprise to you then?"

"No. Not entirely. When she disappeared, I naturally assumed she'd gone to him. Well, it's natural, isn't it? Part of me thought it would just be a short *affaire*. Not that I'll ever know now."

He lapsed into silence and sat staring into space, his face bleak. Beyond the walls of the flat, Thomas could hear the hum of the late afternoon traffic. On the mantlepiece opposite he saw a framed photograph. Finishing his drink he stood up to examine it.

"How long ago was this taken?

"Oh, about eight years ago. We were on holiday in Toulouse."

"This is your daughter?"

"Yes, she was thirteen then."

"A pretty thing."

"Isn't she?"

"She still lives with you?"

"No, I live alone now, at present. She's in England at the moment. Teaching."

Thomas continued to scrutinize the photograph. The woman who stood next to Le Conte was tall and beautiful, possessing that classical elegance which French women often had. There was a faraway look in her eyes as if she wished she were elsewhere.

"Can I take this with me?" he asked.

"Of course. I suppose I shall have to identify the body?"

"I'm afraid so Monsieur. I can arrange transport for you."

"I'll inform the university then."

Thomas stared down into the street below. Sunlight burnished the tops of the cars and passersby hurried to and fro, trying to escape the harsh glare. On the corner a solitary news vendor shouted out the details of some sensational murder. He glanced back at the photograph. A happy family once. Like any other. How deceptive appearances could be.

CHAPTER SEVEN
LOST SOULS

He had made a real effort with the flat. Three substantial table lamps had replaced the stark overhead lighting, and in the centre of the room, over the old pine boards, lay a large Afghan rug, which had set him back £200 from the market in Corn Street. The removal men, who had arrived shortly after his return from the massage parlour in Easton, the previous afternoon, had been quick and efficient and by late evening his few possessions were in place. First out of the boxes was his record collection and player, next the fine glassware his mother had given him.

By the time the doorbell rang at eight that evening the wine was well aired and the lasagna smelled delicious, even if he said so himself.

He opened the flat door. Frances smiled at him. She looked stunning in a low cut, long black dress. Her blonde hair shone in the hall light and there was a faint smell of roses about her. She clutched a bottle of red wine, nervously.

"Come in," he said. "I'm really glad you could make it."

He led the way into the living room.

"Drink?"

"Yes please. Looks as if you've settled in."

"I have."

94

She perched on the edge of the sofa, crossing her long legs as he busied himself with the wine.

"We had a rug like this in our old house in Manaccan," she said when he returned with the wine. "It's in Cornwall. On the Lizard." she continued.

Bottrell stared in amazement.

"What a coincidence!" he exclaimed. "I know it so well! That's where I lived as a boy. On the Lizard. I'm afraid it's been a long while since I've been there. Too long!"

"You should go back. It's an amazing county, isn't it? More coastline than any other in Britain. I so miss the sea."

"I know. Your folks still live there?"

"Only my mother now. Though not in the big house. She has a small cottage down in West Penwith. We still go down a lot, when my father isn't working. I was brought up in Cornwall. It was my playground as a child." she said.

"Me too. What brought you eastwards then?"

"No work there. Cornwall's fine for tourism and the service industries, but not much else."

"That's true."

"When my father got a job at Bristol University we upped sticks and moved. We still go back there for holidays though, as I said. My mother prefers it down there. I'm going down in a few weeks' time, as a matter of fact. You should come down."

"On the Great Western Railway."

"Well on British Rail, yes!" she laughed.

"I might take you up on that."

Over the lasagna they chatted about the Bedminster case.

"Do you have any leads yet?" Frances asked.

"Not exactly. We interviewed the girlfriend, but she was pretty unforthcoming. She put us on to an old rival of Kevin

Saunders, Roy N'como. He's a heavy who runs a massage parlour in Easton."

"You think they were revenge killings?"

"I'm pretty sure they were. What do you think?"

"Yes, I tend to agree, but there's something Walker pointed out this morning you should know about."

"Oh yes?"

"He had a look at the insect evidence. It appears that the eggs and larvae on each corpse were at different stages of growth."

"Meaning that they were murdered at different times —"

"Or in different places where there were differing temperatures. Unfortunately he can't be precise as to when or where."

"And they were murdered by different people?"

"That's possible. Also one of them was left-handed, the other right-handed."

"But you think their murders were connected?" He was intrigued.

"I'm sure of it. I'm just not sure of the link."

There was a silence. Frances shivered.

"You find it cold in here?"

"Strangely, yes."

"I'm glad it's not just me."

"What do you mean?"

"I'm afraid to say the flat may be haunted."

"Really?" she said, surprised. "You're not joking are you? You're serious!"

"I thought it might be me overreacting at first. But the girl who lives in the adjacent flat has also experienced things."

"What sort of things?"

"Strange sounds in the night, odd drops in temperature."

"You believe in ghosts?" She smiled.

"I'm not sure," he said. "I seem to have an instinct for things unseen. My mother had it too. As for ghosts, I have a theory about that."

"Oh yes?"

"I believe what Einstein has to say about time. If time is relative, past and present can exist in parallel. Maybe when some people see ghosts they're glimpsing another dimension."

"That's an interesting theory. But what about life after death?"

"The survival of bodily death? Sure. Why not? Why shouldn't the mind be capable of some sort of independent existence? Otherwise how else do we explain OBEs?"

"What?"

"Out of Body Experiences – near death experiences – and telepathic communication. There has to be a rational explanation for such things."

"But we have no proof the mind can survive death. The only reality we have is what we perceive through the mechanisms of the human mind."

"I suppose a psychologist would say that."

"I guess so. Don't get me wrong, John. I don't altogether discount the possibility of life after death. I just don't have any proof, that's all.

"Neither do I, but proof isn't everything."

Frances left at around eleven thirty. Still elated by her company, Bottrell cleared away the empty dishes, then poured himself a whisky and stood by the living room window, staring out into the garden below. The sun had long gone and the garden was quiet and dark. A sudden feeling of fatigue overcame him. He moved into the bedroom and, putting his glass on the bedside table, lay down on the bed and closed his eyes. Soon he was asleep.

He was in a hospital corridor. Bristol Infirmary. It was late at night and the place was virtually deserted. He walked through a set of double doors and, turning left, found the ward he was looking for. His brother, Hugh, lay in a bed in the intensive care unit, his face deathly pale, a white plastic tube filling his mouth. He had lain like this for days, not moving, scarcely breathing, hovering between life and death.

Bottrell stooped over the bed and whispered his name, "Hugh," but there was no response. He stretched out his hand and grasped his brother's fingers but they were cold to the touch, cold as death. He glanced round the room, then through the doors into the ward beyond. Nothing stirred there. The patients lay in their beds, not moving, cradled in sleep. It seemed as if he was standing in the house of the dead.

The suffocating odour of ethanol began to fill the room. Claustrophobic, he walked from the room into the silent ward but he had got no further than the other side of the double doors when he heard his brother's voice, calling his name. He turned and stared through at the limp, rag doll's body, the eyes saucers of sorrow, the hands outstretched. He tried to call out to Hugh but no sound came from his lips and he was rooted to the spot. Then, like a black veil, the darkness descended…

He woke in a sweat. Far off, as if in another room, he could hear the sound of a woman's voice, weeping.

The Bureau was on the top floor of a large, imposing building in the Boulevard de la Tour Maubourg, close by the Place des Invalides. The temperature on the street was probably in the upper 80s, the brick buildings reflecting the heat like a great oven as DC Thomas climbed the steps and entered through the heavy stained-glass doors. When he discovered the ancient lift was broken, he cursed loudly and slowly made his way up the ten sets of stairs, pausing often to catch his breath and wipe his forehead.

Inspector Paul Le Coq was in the process of finishing a large Havana cigar when Thomas entered. He was not alone. Seated at their desks was an array of burly colleagues, banging away at their typewriters, answering the telephone or chatting with each other.

A short, dapper man with a thin pencil moustache, Le Coq was a veteran of the Sûreté who, over a period of twenty years, had gained an encyclopedic knowledge of the criminal underworld of his native Paris.

"Monsieur Thomas. Good to meet you. *ça va?*"

"I'm well thank you, except for this intolerable heat."

"Ah, that we have no control over. You asked me to check a name for you."

"Indeed I did."

"And I have done so. Isabelle Le Conte, reported missing in July 1972 by her husband, Jean Le Conte. The case was never resolved."

"Was there liaison with the British authorities?"

"Yes there was some initial contact with your British police force. The husband was of the opinion that she had left France to live with her English lover but we had no proof that it was so."

"Did you interview the husband?"

"Not me. The interview was conducted by – let me see." He leafed through the file on his desk. "By Jacques Viand of the Montmartre district. You are aware, I suppose, that the husband was reported to us about a year before Isabelle Le Conte's disappearance?"

"Is that so?"

"Yes, I have the report here. The police were called to the *appartement* in the Rue Huysmans on April 3rd 1971. They found the wife in a state of distress. There had been a fight and the wife – she said she had been beaten. She had medical treatment for cuts and bruises to her face, arms and shoulders. She was interviewed twice by Jacques Viand but she decided not to go further." He shrugged.

Thomas reflected for a moment as Le Coq stubbed out the remains of his cigar.

"You say you found her remains in Bristol?" Le Coq continued, leaning back in his chair and eyeing his visitor quizzically.

"So we did."

"And what – you think maybe the lover killed her?"

"We don't know. So far we haven't traced him."

"So listen – what if the husband came over to England, found her, they quarrelled and he killed her?"

"It's a possibility."

"You've spoken to the husband. How does he seem?"

"Difficult to say. A little detached maybe. One thing which gives me cause for concern though. When I told him about his wife's death he seemed to accept it too easily. I was not convinced at his pretence of grief. And it seems that he only pursued her disappearance for a short time. Too short."

"So this file would suggest. He will accompany you to England, to identify her body?"

"Yes. He returns to England tomorrow."

"Then good luck with your case, my friend. Oh, one other thing which may be of interest. Isabelle was married before to an artist in Normandy, a Henri Fleur. I'll give you the address."

* * *

100

David Gould had retired three years ago from the Avon and Somerset Police. A stout, florid-faced man with greying hair and chiselled features, he lived alone in a large house in St Mary's Road, on the edge of Leigh Woods, where he devoted much of his time to his twin pleasures of gardening and beekeeping. Despite his retirement from active police work, he continued to follow the details of the most significant murder cases in the Bristol area with undiminished interest, and the discovery of the bodies of Kevin Saunders and Michael Aswere held special interest for him, not least because he had been personally involved with both of them prior to their disappearance. He was therefore unsurprised to find Bottrell and Evans appearing unannounced in his driveway early one Sunday morning. Hearing the unhealthy rattle of their Ford Escort, he closed the top of the hive and walked back to the house, still swathed in his beekeeper's outfit.

"David Gould?" asked Bottrell.

Gould removed one of his gauntlets and shook his hand.

"The same. And you gentlemen are?"

Bottrell and Evans produced their warrant cards.

"DCs Bottrell and Evans."

"Come inside and tell me what this is all about."

Ex-DCI Gould, a policeman of the old school, was a man who had always believed in the link between bonhomie and strong drink. As Bottrell and Evans entered the mock-Tudor living room, therefore, he had already made his way to the drinks cabinet and, discarding his protective suit, now stood with an expectant look on his face, like some ageing bartender.

"Drinks?" he enquired.

"Make mine a soft drink – orange juice or something," Bottrell replied.

"Me too," said Evans. "It's far too early for me."

Gould poured two glasses of orange into long tumblers, then helped himself to a double malt, before sprawling into a chair.

"I find this stuff revives the flagging memory," he observed. "I suppose you're on duty, though."

"We are," Bottrell replied. "We've come to ask you about two characters you would have had dealings with on your watch in 1972: Kevin Saunders and Michael Aswere."

"Names forever printed into the little grey cells," Gould joked. He was grinning now but there was no trace of warmth behind the eyes. He reached into his trouser pocket and, producing a packet of cigarettes, lit one, then offered them to his visitors. Bottrell lit his, the cheap tobacco tearing the back of his throat like glass paper. He stubbed it out.

"Kevin Saunders was well known on my manor since he robbed a mini supermarket on the Bedminster estate where he lived. That was at the tender age of fourteen. From that he progressed to burglary, assault and, of course, drugs."

"What about the other one, Michael Aswere?" asked Evans.

"Sure. I knew him well. These two were firm buddies. Partners in crime you might say. Kevin's father was a real piece of work. A powerful well-built West Indian with a vicious temper. Used to beat his son with a studded belt, right up to the age of fourteen, so I gather. Not that it made much difference of course. Michael came from a more privileged background. Came over from the West Indies with his family. His father was a high ranking diplomat, his mother a woman from the Congo. Michael got his looks from her. But he was bad seed. Got done for shoplifting at sixteen and by seventeen was conducting a protection racket among the younger boys at his school. I always said he was the brains behind the outfit. It was Michael who got

Kevin into the drugs racket. They started in a small way at first, supplying small amounts of cannabis resin to the local schools. Then they got into contact with a Mr Big and set up an import business from Jamaica. They had a number of stool pigeons working for them. We knew their names but never had enough evidence to convict. You sure you don't want a proper drink?"

Bottrell shook his head.

"What we're trying to determine is whether either of them had put anyone's nose out of joint sufficiently that they may have had cause to murder them."

"You mean someone from a rival gang?"

"Something like that, yes. Someone with a big enough grudge."

"What you've got to understand is that there really was no rival gang who could take them on, that is. There were individuals of course who may have harboured a grudge."

"Roy N'como, for instance?"

There was a pause. Then Gould said:

"It's interesting you should mention his name. I had a couple of run-ins with N'como in the early 70s. He was running a number of prostitutes in the Easton area at the time. We were called to a house one night. Turned out some city type had died during a bondage session there. We found out later he was supplying over half the cocaine in the Bristol area. He might have had cause."

Bottrell produced a photograph, which he placed on the coffee table. Gould leaned forward to examine it.

"I've seen this many times," he said.

"What is it exactly?" asked Bottrell.

"SCB. Street Cred Boys. It's a gang some of the lads belonged to in Bedminster. A lot of them had the tattoo from Jamaica. There was a gang there who armed themselves and committed a number of robberies. They were disbanded in 1971 by the Jamaican police. You know, I suppose, that both Saunders and Aswere were importing firearms through Bristol airport?"

"We did know that," said Evans. "We suspected that N'como was also running a similar racket. In fact I've heard say that he's still at it."

"If they were in competition with each other, it might provide a motive," observed Evans.

"Maybe. N'como is a tragic figure really."

"Oh, why's that?"

"He lost his six year old son in a car accident. A hit and run. We never found out who did it. There were two witnesses to the incident – young boys – but neither of them would give evidence. Too afraid. But someone on that estate knew who it was. Another drink then?"

"No thanks," said Bottrell, standing up. "We must be going."

"People to see, collars to feel, I know," Gould joked. "You should retire and try beekeeping. It's a lot more satisfying."

"I'm sure it would be."

They moved into the hallway, where a light breeze from the door lifted the heat from their faces.

"Oh, one thing before you go, gentlemen. This French student who's been murdered. It rang a bell when I read about it in the newspaper. About ten years back there was a woman attacked on the Downs. She was a prostitute called Amy Styles. She'd been working the toilets near the old water tower. She'd gone into some bushes and had just finished with a client when someone attacked her from behind with a knife. Stabbed her several times and left her for dead. I don't know if it's the same pattern?"

"I wasn't aware of this case," replied Bottrell. "Did she see her attacker's face?"

"No she didn't get a chance, though she said she thought her attacker was a shortish person. When she collapsed, she blacked out. She was lucky to survive. The punter she'd been with heard her screams and came back. Otherwise she would have died."

Bottrell made a note of the name in his pocket book.

"You've been most helpful," he said, shaking Gould's hand.

Gould smiled back at them.

"Don't suppose I can tempt either of you to a jar of honey before you go?" he asked.

The two men made their escape.

"Lonely man, I think." said Evans.

Bottrell nodded sadly.

"Whisky at that hour of the morning! It's a shame to see a good policeman go down that path."

They drove in silence back over the suspension bridge.

CHAPTER EIGHT
TROUVILLE

Trouville lay on the Normandy coast, a few miles from the port of Le Havre. By the time that Thomas arrived in the mid-afternoon, the town's promenade and its tangle of bustling pedestrian streets were alive with summer holidaymakers. Thomas parked his hire car outside the spectacular Victorian frontage of L'Hotel des Roches Noires and stood for a moment, gazing up at its ornate brickwork and turrets, then wove his way along the promenade.

The beach was a forest of small families enjoying the sea, whilst the baking streets teemed with street traders and half-dressed day trippers, eating ice creams. Pausing to consult his map beneath the shade of a hotel awning, he discovered that Henri Fleur lived in the Rue Cachin, a long terraced street to the south of the town. Despite the intense heat of the afternoon, he decided he would walk the quarter of a mile rather than be shut inside an airless taxi. He made his way through narrow, twisting streets, filled with old mansions, until at last the houses gave way on one side to a stretch of meadow and on the other, a set of sober, yellow-bricked villas. At number 65 he stopped and, passing through a low gate, half off its hinges, knocked on the door. There was a long pause, then the door opened. A tall, powerfully built man of about forty stood in the doorway. His grey, receding hair was pulled back into a ponytail. He had a long, sensitive face with deep set blue eyes and his skin was burnished by constant exposure to sea and sun. He was dressed in an old pair of khaki shorts and a paint-stained T-shirt. There was something very bohemian about him, Thomas thought.

"Henri Fleur?" he asked, politely.

"Oui. C'est moi."

Thomas produced his warrant card and Fleur invited him inside. He was relieved to discover that the interior of the villa was surprisingly cool, a gentle breeze wafting through from the French windows at the back. He looked around the room. Every inch of wall space was covered with a series of unframed oil paintings. The style was rough and muscular, the paintings showing large landscapes of the Normandy countryside along with an occasional female nude.

"So. What does an Englishman want with Henri Fleur?"

The Frenchman smiled and Thomas felt instantly at ease. There was something about the man that cut through formality and encouraged him to relax. He wondered why Isabelle Le Conte would have left this man for the less than inspiring Jean. He felt intrigued.

"Want to buy a painting?" Fleur asked, grinning.

"That depends on the price," he replied, entering into the spirit of the thing.

"I'm not expensive. My reputation as an artist does not extend far out of Normandy, monsieur. I'm drinking calvados. Would you care to join me?"

He reached up to a large pine dresser and, polishing a glass with a less than clean handkerchief, filled it to the brim. Thomas winced.

"Now then," said Fleur, perching on a wooden stool by the window. "Perhaps you would tell me what you are doing here?"

Thomas downed the calvados in one go, assuaging his thirst, but immediately regretted it as his head began to swim.

"I believe you were once married to Isabelle Le Conte," he said.

"I was indeed. I was married to her for four years. Four good years. She lived with me here in Trouville. Why? What has happened?"

"I'm afraid she's been murdered."

Fleur put down his glass and ran a hand through his hair.

"I don't believe it! She was such fun... and so beautiful. This is terrible news. I wondered what had happened to her. Has Jean Le Conte been told?"

"Yes." replied Thomas. He's travelling to England to identify her remains."

"Remains? Why is that? Her body do you mean?"

"I'm sorry, Monsieur. When the body was discovered she'd been dead about four years. We have had great difficulty in identifying her."

Fleur looked visibly shocked.

"*Pauvre Isabelle*. Left for four years. So you are here for what?"

"To find out as much information about her as possible."

"Of course! Pardon... How did you find me?"

"Through the Bureau in Paris."

"She was murdered? Who murdered her?"

"We don't know who murdered her. Not yet."

"Where in England was she?"

"In Bristol."

He nodded.

"I know the place. I have contacts in that city."

"Contacts?"

"Fellow artists. I belong to an international collective. We are all expressionist painters. We take our inspiration from Rothko and Munch. Tell me. Why was she in Bristol?"

"We believe she had left her husband and intended to live with a painter called Jack Slade. You know of him?"

"I've not heard of him. From Bristol, you say? Strange. But tell me. How did she die?"

"We believe she was stabbed to death."

Fleur refilled their glasses and reached for a packet of cigarettes.

"You smoke?"

"Thanks."

"This is the worst news," Fleur said. "I had a dream that she had died – about four years ago. It was very real... vivid, do you say? It upset me. I believed it was in my imagination but now I don't think so. In my dream she asked me to look after the child."

"The child? Her daughter, you mean?"

"Isabelle had two daughters, one by this man Le Conte. The other she gave away before she met me, when she lived in Honfleur. With her mother. She was young. Seventeen. Then it was very hard to have a child with no husband. You understand? Her mother said she must give it away. It was adopted by an English couple. They spent their *vacances* each year with the Giscards – that was Isabelle's name then. The husband was Ecosse, I think – what do you say?"

"Scottish."

"Yes. Scottish."

"What was the name?"

"I do not recollect. They took the child to England. She didn't see her after that. It was tragic. There was something in

Isabelle. Some deep sadness. *Tres triste.* I could never find why. You know about her father?"

"No."

"He was a fisherman, working at Honfleur. He died of poisoning from the food when he was still young. He was a beast of a man. He beat Isabelle. He beat her mother too. All the time. People talked about the mother. They called her 'La Sorciere' and said she had given him poison. I did not think so. We could never have children and Isabelle was very sad about this. I think she blamed me, never forgave me."

"Why did she leave you?"

"We argued. It was a *grand passion* – a lot of love but too much fighting. She thought I was too attentive, did not give her room. I just loved her that's all. She was a free spirit and an artist. Better than me. But she could never work at it for long. She should have stayed here... She would have been happier than..."

He tailed off and stared thoughtfully into space.

"Happier than what?" asked Thomas.

"Happier than with Le Conte."

"What do you mean?"

"He was never right for her. Cold. Passionless. Good with his head but not his heart. You understand what I mean? She was never happy with him. Never. He could be cruel too. You know that she left him and came back to live here with me. Lived here for six months. Arrived at my house – June 1970. I think he had done something to her but she would not tell me. Kept it close to her heart. She would have stayed for good if her other daughter had not turned up and begged her to go back. Another calvados, monsieur?"

Thomas politely declined. He was already feeling the effects of his first glass.

"You've met Jean Le Conte?" Fleur continued. "What did you think?"

"A little distant – and as you said, cold. Self-contained."

"Oui! That's him. He liked to control people. He did that with Isabelle too. Emptied her of life. What is the word?"

"Stifled?" added Thomas, helpfully.

"Stifled. Yes. I'm glad she quit him. I'm sorry this has happened to her. Very sorry. Why were her 'remains' there so long?"

"The body had been hidden away."

"But Le Conte. He must have searched for her, oui?"

"He assumed she was with her painter from Bristol."

Fleur frowned.

"Something is not right. Yes? Maybe she did not go back to see this man? Maybe she wanted to find her daughter? Who knows?"

A silence descended in the room. Far off, Thomas could hear the screeching of gulls, such a haunting sound. He felt sorry for the French woman, sorry for Henri Fleur, sorry for the relationship which had gone wrong. He sighed. He finished his drink and stood up, swaying slightly from the calvados.

"Anyway, Monsieur Fleur, I must be going. I have a long drive back to Paris."

"Wait! I must show you this." replied Fleur.

He went to the pine dresser and, opening a drawer, pulled out a small photograph. The print showed a tall, elegant woman with dark hair sitting on the beach. Next to her was an older woman who resembled her, also with dark hair. In the foreground, sitting on a blanket, was a very small, plump child with dark eyes.

"This is Isabelle with her mother and her little girl. Taken a long time before I met her. It is the only one I have. You can take it." He smiled in farewell. "*Bon voyage*, Mr Thomas."

Outside, Thomas stopped at the corner of the street and gazed at the photo again. Maybe Fleur was right. Maybe he should check out Le Conte's story more thoroughly. He would phone Glenister in the morning and ask if they had made any progress in contacting Slade. On the other hand, did Slade actually exist? Surely Fleur would have heard of him through his international group? Had Le Conte made him up? It was conceivable. He crossed the street, stepping once more into the hot July sunshine. Far off, he could hear the sounds of the holidaymakers and the shrieks of the children playing on the beach. He walked back in the direction of the town, thinking of the woman in the photograph and the curly haired child at her feet. For some inexplicable reason, a feeling of immense sadness overwhelmed him.

* * *

Norman Stanton stood outside Ronald Savageri's office, nervously picking his fingers. A band of perspiration dappled his lined forehead and he blinked rapidly behind the heavy black glasses. He knocked again but there was no answer. Just then Sally Acre appeared at the end of the corridor and hailed him cheerfully.

"Mr Stanton. Do go in. Mr Savageri won't be long. He's just popped to the loo."

Stanton opened the door and entered. The room was airless and smelled strongly of sweat. He went over to the window and opened it wide, letting in a gust of traffic fumes and hot, stifling air.

Stanton was a fastidious man who abhorred the natural functions of the human body. That was partly why he had never considered marriage or the possibility of a long term relationship with a woman. It was not that he found the female form revolting. He preferred to view women from afar and, if contact were to be made, it was only virginal flesh that satisfied his cravings. Young and pure and clean. He had spent most of his forty-nine years observing the female body and it was for this very reason that he had been attracted to teaching, to be in the company of young women.

A door opened at the end of the corridor and Savageri appeared, hot and bothered, shuffling towards him, his large face wet with perspiration.

"Ah, Mr Stanton. A word please."

Savageri shut the door firmly and Stanton's heart sank. A private talk was the last thing he wanted. His face drained of colour. Ever since he had arrived at work this morning he had feared the summons to the principal's office. He had overstepped the mark. He knew it. He had known it the moment she had slapped his face in the bedroom of his flat in Clifton.

Her name was Antoinette and she was one of the more mature-looking students. She came from Picardy and her parents were wealthy hoteliers. Her long fair hair and soft peach-like complexion excited him. Her smooth skin was ripe for stroking. Smooth and hairless and sweet-smelling. For a girl of just sixteen she was well proportioned with large breasts and long, slender legs. The moment he had spotted her in the language school reception area he had hoped and prayed that she would be placed in one of his classes and his prayers had been answered.

Antoinette was a gregarious girl who learned quickly and it was not long before he had offered the advantage of his 'extra-curricular' classes, as he called them. This was not the first time he had attempted to 'cultivate' one of his female students. The previous summer he had sustained a three week affair with a girl from Brittany and had managed to swear her to secrecy. Unfortunately Savageri had found out about it and had given him a warning.

However, Antoinette was no pushover. An independent-minded girl, she had mistakenly assumed Stanton's intentions had been completely harmless. But an afternoon in his flat had soon laid bare his real intentions and his appearance in the living room, dressed only in a short towelling robe, had not produced the reaction he had so wanted. When he had approached her, flattered her and then had tried to kiss her, she had slapped his face and stormed out of the flat, threatening to contact the police about his behaviour.

In reality she had done nothing of the kind. He had spent an anxious night, barely sleeping, waiting for that knock on the door. Instead, she had complained to her host parents, the Reverend Halbett and his wife. They had been horrified and had contacted the police themselves.

"It really won't do, Stanton," said Savageri, shuffling the papers on his desk. "It's not as if this is the first time I've received a complaint about you. And please don't try to excuse yourself. There *is* no excuse. Don't take me for a fool."

Stanton took off his spectacles, rubbed the lenses, then placed them back on the bridge of his nose.

"Look, can't you just speak to Antoinette? Speak to her host parents perhaps?"

His voice was weak and plaintive.

Savageri frowned.

"I'm afraid it's gone too far this time," he said. "The police are now involved. I warned you last summer that if this happened again I would not be able to protect you from the consequences of your actions. I might say your timing is appalling, all things considered."

"What things?" he asked, faintly.

"Rachael La Mer, for Christ's sake. Do you really think they won't make some sort of connection?"

Stanton went cold with fear.

"I hadn't thought. I hadn't imagined..." he stammered.

"I'm sorry Norman, but you leave me no option in the matter. I shall have to insist on your suspension forthwith, until the governors can look into the affair. We cannot countenance this sort of behaviour. We are here to protect these young people, not abuse them. And you'd better prepare yourself for a visit from the police. Please close the door when you leave."

* * *

Bottrell had been walking for some time now. His journey had taken him south from his flat down to the tree-lined avenue of St Andrew's cemetery. It was early morning and the sun was just edging its way over the eastern horizon. He needed to walk, to clear his head, to breathe again. The intense heat of the past few days had taken its toll and his head felt as if it were encased in cotton wool. The dry air and desiccated streets of the city had become like a prison, threatening to suffocate him. But at this early hour the roads were quiet and the city had not yet sprung to life. As he passed through the old churchyard and exited onto Clifton Hill, he could hear a chorus of bird song. It filled the air and his spirits lightened immediately. He thought of Cornwall.

When he reached the top of Constitution Hill, he paused for a moment and stared out across the city where red-bricked Victorian villas jostled for space with large skyscrapers and derricks, a dark tableau cast against a red sky. As he descended

115

the hill, he reflected on the previous night's events. He had returned to the flat hot and weary and somewhat disconsolate at the lack of progress in the Bedminster case. Anne Marie had been standing on the staircase and had seemed eager to speak to him.

"Anne Marie?"

"John – could you spare me some time?"

He was in no mood to do anything other than crash on his sofa and sleep but when he saw her face generosity got the better of him. Sitting in her living room was a tall, angular-faced woman with jet black hair and piercing blue eyes.

"This is Diana – Diana Seaton. She's a friend of mine."

"Good to meet you."

"Diana is a medium. She has come to help me. I thought, John, maybe you could be here too?"

"Sensing her awkwardness, Bottrell interceded.

"You are a spiritualist?"

The woman nodded.

"A Christian spiritualist. Anne Marie tells me you have an unquiet spirit here in the house."

"It would appear so."

"An unhappy soul we may be able to put to rest."

"Maybe so," Bottrell replied.

Sensing his reserve, the woman stared at him sharply.

"You have reservations?"

"I like to keep an open mind about such things."

There was a silence.

"John, if you're not happy with this…?" said Anne Marie.

"No, no, let's do this. We should give it a go."

"Very well then," said Diana, "let's proceed."

She stood up and, drawing the curtains, lit a large white candle which she placed in the centre of the drop-leaf table.

Anne Marie sat down next to Diana and the medium closed her eyes. The three held hands. There was a long silence. Bottrell watched the medium's impassive face. Then, slowly, her forehead furrowed and her mouth tightened.

"Cold – cold – too long here – please help me —" she exclaimed. The voice was thin and reedy with a faint west country accent. Anne Marie's hand tightened its grip.

"Who are you?" asked Bottrell. "Please tell us your name."

There was a pause.

"Christine. My name is Christine."

"How long have you been here, Christine?"

"Too long. Too long. Trapped here. Suffocating... You must help me..."

"When did you live here, Christine? How long ago?"

"Can't move. Can't breathe. Don't know. So long..."

The medium's breathing was rapid now, the voice loud and piercing. Her shoulders were shaking with the sustained effort, her head bent over the table.

"She is with me, she has me still. I'm her prisoner. Can't leave. Please help... please..."

"Who is this? Who's holding you? Tell us," urged Bottrell.

The medium moaned, then slumped forward onto the table, sobbing, her shoulders convulsed. Bottrell released his hand from Anne Marie, who was rigid with tension, and placed a reassuring hand on Diana's shoulder.

"Is she OK? Is she alright?" asked Anne Marie anxiously.

Bottrell placed his finger to his lips.

"Give her a moment," he said quietly. "She'll come round in a minute."

Slowly the medium's breathing became more regular. She opened her eyes and sat up, looking confused.

"OK, Diana?" he said at last.

"Yes, I'm alright. What happened?"

Bottrell explained.

"There's something very wrong here," she said. "A woman's spirit trapped in these walls. I don't understand why. It's as if her physical presence is still here. I'm not sure I can do any more to help you."

"Not to worry," he reassured her. "You tried."

* * *

Bottrell had turned into Jacobs Wells Road now and was drawing level with the old police station. His mind went back to when he was a child. One day his father had taken him to the docks.

They had crossed over the harbour onto Merchant's Quay and there they had stopped and stared into a deep cave in the limestone rock.

"You see this place?" asked his father. "This is where the slaves were kept. The merchant ships would embark here and the slaves would be pushed in here, in chains, thirty or forty of them at a time, kept in the dark without food or water for days at a time. If they complained, they'd be beaten."

He remembered how it had felt. A great well of suffering, trapped here for centuries, a chorus of voices still echoing against the damp, limestone walls. Even after all this time, their suffering was still tangible, still audible to him. For the remainder of that day the memory had haunted him, disturbed him. That same tangibility was evident in Anne Marie's flat in the tortured spasms of the medium. You could almost taste it.

Turning into Cannon's Road, he drew level with the harbour and stood at the railings, smelling the fresh morning breeze. The place was silent save for a few early vagrants and three or four barges slowly making their way upstream. Two hundred years ago the dock would have been alive with slave ships, disgorging their doomed cargo, teeming with slave masters and wealthy merchants, a place of suffering, greed and sorrow. Now it was but a ghost of its former imperial past, haunted by the whispers of lost souls.

He found a coffee bar by College Green and ordered an espresso. By now the traffic had begun to thunder down Park Street and the pavements were busy with early morning commuters. He downed his coffee and crossed the Green, heading for the imposing Edwardian facade of Bristol Central Library.

Inside it was cool and inviting. He climbed the great steps and found himself in the oak-lined reference library with its smell of wax and leather-bound tomes. He scanned the local history section. *History of the British Slave Trade*, *The Merchant Venturers*, *St Mary Redcliffe*. It was an impressive collection.

Then a small, quarto edition caught his eye. *Murder and Mayhem in Victorian Bristol*. He found a spare reading desk and sat back in the padded chair to consult its index. Under 'P' he soon found what he was looking for: Pembroke Road. He turned to page 123. 'The Pembroke Road Murder'.

He read on: 'In the July of 1876, the citizens of Bristol were horrified to learn of the discovery of a woman's body in a house in the fashionable part of the city. The body was discovered in a large pine trunk which had lain in the attic of one of the large Victorian mansions in Pembroke Road. Mr George Filby, a Bristol businessman, had purchased the house and moved in with his family early in the July of 1876. After some days, Mr Filby's wife had become aware of an unpleasant odour which came from the top floor of the building. Upon investigation the smell was traced to a large seaman's chest which lay hidden under a piece of canvas. When a crowbar was used to prise open the lid, Mr Filby was horrified to discover the mutilated remains of a young woman. The naked corpse, which had been forced into the trunk, was minus its arms and legs.

'During the course of their investigation, the police discovered that the previous owner, a Monsieur Rousseau, had returned to France a month previously. The French police were contacted and an order issued for Rousseau's extradition. It was later discovered that the murdered woman was a French painter whom he had killed in a fit of rage. The trial of Rousseau took place in the August of 1876 and attracted much interest in the pages of the sensational press. He was sentenced to death and hanged in September 1876'.

Bottrell scanned the article again. The entry was annoyingly brief and did not mention the name of the victim. He would have to examine the newspapers for the period in question. He glanced at his wrist watch. Nine thirty. He would be late for the briefing. Making a few quick notes he closed the book and returned it to the shelf.

CHAPTER NINE
MISSING LINKS

She had grown to hate the old woman. In the beginning, when she had first moved into the Bedminster flat, a young family had bought the flat next to hers and because the mother had been her own age she had struck up a casual friendship. But it was not to last. In October the family moved out and the flat was purchased by Mrs Beddoes. A widow in her early 70s, she was a free spirit and something of a new ager. For a while they rubbed along reasonably well but gradually the woman drove her to distraction. After a while it was obvious she was going to be trouble. Employed as a care worker, she would arrive at odd hours, laden with bags of shopping which she would leave outside her flat door, blocking the shared hall. Mrs Beddoes had two elderly cats, both of them unneutered toms. The old battlers would spray in the hallway or fight continuously outside her front window at dead of night, often when the old woman was working. But it was not just her cats which irritated her. It was the fact that Mrs Beddoes was opinionated and would always go to great lengths to prove her point, always pointing out things that were wrong in the house, always trying to change the way things were run. She could feel her control slipping. She hated to be questioned and criticised. She'd put up with that when she was young, but she vowed never to do that again.

One day she happened to see an advertisement in the local paper asking for host families for French students during the summer months. She applied and was most charming to the woman who came to interview. How easily she could lay on the charm when she needed to.

For some weeks she earned a reasonable income from providing them with bed and board. But that was all they got. She had no interest in them personally at all. She laid down strict rules. They would only be admitted to the flat after 5pm and she had insisted they leave by 8.30am each morning. By lodging two female students in bunk beds in the second bedroom she found she could greatly increase her earning potential. But the scheme foundered when she received a letter from her insurance company, informing her that since she was running a business from her residence she had invalidated her policy.

There was only one person who could have informed them, she was sure of it. That interfering old hag next door. She was furious, and from that point onwards she decided to be rid of Mrs Beddoes. She felt disempowered by what the old woman had done. The flat and the building were hers, her own inner sanctum that she could control. Now she no longer felt safe.

She kept a log of the woman's movements. Each alternate weekend Mrs Beddoes would be absent from the flat. It was then she seized her chance. She waited in the stairwell outside the flat on the Saturday when she knew the house would be empty. The cats would be around for their food, the woman often leaving it in the hall when she was away. Spotting one of the cats, she lured it into her flat using the bowl of food as bait, grabbed it and trussed it in a blanket. Then she took it in the car to a canal some miles from the city. She had grappled with the struggling cat, holding it in the blanket between her knees and had cut a piece of fur from its back before binding it tightly in the blanket once again and hurling it into the dark, oily waters. She carefully placed the piece of fur in her purse. It would join her collection. The second cat had escaped her, scratching her hand badly. Each time she tried to catch it the vile thing had growled fiercely and fled.

On the Sunday she waited in her flat, listening for the old lady's return. Around 3am she heard the front door open. The old woman's movements were predictable. She would sleep for a few hours, rise at 9am and busy herself in the flat. She could hear every sound the woman made through the thin walls. She would spend hours with her ear glued to the wall when Mrs Beddoes was in, logging her movements. Later the old woman would go to her church, about ten minutes away, to commune with her god. Once she had left she got to work. She began washing the stairs.

This was her weekly ritual. She would spend hours scrubbing the stone stairs and landing. Other residents would often complain about it but she would merely glare at them and slam the door. Sometimes she would simply not answer the door at all, but press herself against the inside of it and listen. One resident had shouted at her through the letterbox, but she simply ignored it and just withdrew into herself.

Normally she would just use bleach and hot water but today she added a quantity of olive oil to the mixture. Today the resultant liquid was soapy and viscous. When she had finished she sat in her usual position behind her flat door and listened. Predictable as ever, the front door opened and Mrs Beddoes began to climb the stairs. She could hear the old woman panting her way up the steps, grumbling under her breath, complaining about the state of the place. There was a sudden cry and the sound of a body hitting the concrete steps hard. Mrs Beddoes lay at the bottom of the stairs moaning but no one came to help her. The flats were all empty save for two. By early afternoon the moaning had ceased. She opened her door and peered cautiously down at the motionless body. The floor and steps were dry. She would see to that later. Gingerly, she made her way down the stairs. It wouldn't do for her to slip as well. The old woman was still breathing but it would not be too long... Picking her way back up to her flat, she smiled with pleasure. She had only just closed the door of her flat when she heard the sound of someone entering the house...

The old woman had lived but her injuries were such that she never returned to her flat. There was some confusion as to how the accident had happened but, since the woman was elderly and the hallway was poorly lit, nothing had come of it. Her surviving cat was taken away by the RSPCA.

She was very careful to remove all trace of the oil on the stairs and as she scrubbed she felt at peace. Tranquility and order had returned and that which she had lost became her own again.

* * *

The Paris to London flight had been delayed. For several hours DC Thomas found himself sitting in the lounge at Charles De Gaulle airport, attempting to read *Le Monde*, but with limited success. In the end he had to admit defeat and gave up in frustration. He imagined Le Conte, who had travelled on an earlier flight, was probably in Bristol now. He waited, seated between a mother with two noisy children and a snoring businessman, thinking about what Fleur had told him.

It was now imperative that he get back to England and discover the truth about Isabelle and Jack Slade. Although he had left messages with Glenister about tracking him down, as yet he had had no affirmative replies.

They were now almost a week into the inquiry and no further near a solution. Finally, at just before 11am, the airport tannoy announced the rescheduled departure of his plane from Gate 7. He made a quick trip to the cafe, purchased two croissants, then grabbed his suitcase and made his way to passport controls.

The small plane touched down just after midday. It had been a hot and uncomfortable trip for him. He'd been placed next to an extremely overweight man who smelled badly and who'd clearly been drinking heavily. His fellow passenger spent the entire trip snoring and occasionally passing wind, much to the discomfiture of the woman in front.

He immediately phoned Glenister upon landing. Glenister then told him of the Language School murder and of the lead they were pursuing. One of the host parents had complained about a member of staff at the Belmont Language School and they intended to interview him. As yet, however, the Bedminster double murder case had yielded no real results, despite Bottrell and Evans's best efforts.

Glenister had contacted the Bristol Academy of Art regarding the whereabouts of Jack Slade. According to their records, he had died of lung cancer in 1973. The last known address for him had turned out to be a flat above a butcher's shop off the Cheltenham Road. They believed he was married at the time of his death but did not have an address for his widow. Tired and tetchy, he told Thomas to get himself over to the Central Library and sort out the Slade contact.

Thomas was weary and annoyed. He knew better than to argue with his boss when he was like this. He'd had no time to draw breath after his journey but he headed across the river onto

College Green. Here he paused to grab a sandwich from a tired-looking street vendor and devoured it hungrily before wearily climbing the great steps of the Reference Library where he consulted a telephone directory for the years 1972 and 1973.

There were six Slades listed, three who bore the initial 'J'. He asked for a copy of the electoral register for 1975. The two Slades listed were a John Eric Slade and a Jacqueline Slade. He cursed under his breath. He would just have to try phoning through the list and see what happened.

Before he left, he asked at the desk for information about Jack Slade. The librarian disappeared for a few moments, then returned bearing a loose leaf folder marked 'Contemporary Bristol Artists'. He leafed through its contents.

'Slade, Jack. Born 1923 in Weston-super-Mare. Educated: Goldsmith College of Art. First exhibited at the Clarkson Gallery, Brook Street, London 1948. Work influenced by the expressionist school. Specialised in landscape and portrait painting. Died Bristol 1973 after a short illness'.

Rather brief, he thought. And no mention of a wife or children. He returned the folder and made his way out into the bright sunshine.

There was a phone box on the corner of College Green, just next to the County Hall building. Seeing it was free, he took out his notebook and started dialling through the six numbers. The first was an elderly woman who could not hear him properly and proceeded to shout at him down the phone. Hastily he replaced the receiver. The second number rang but there was no answer. The third rang for a while, then was picked up by a child whose mother, alarmingly, was out at work and wouldn't be back until teatime. But on the fourth attempt he struck lucky. A woman's voice answered. Yes, she did know of a Jack Slade. He had been her husband. Who was this? Thomas explained. What was the enquiry about? She sounded guarded. Could he speak to her in person? When might be convenient – this afternoon? Reluctantly, the voice on the end of the phone consented. Half-past four, 28, Marlborough Street, just off Marlborough Road. Flat Six.

Hazel Slade occupied a flat in a tall, art deco house just past the Bristol Royal Infirmary. The building, which had seen better days, stood at the end of a terraced row and was fronted by a set of rusting railings. Its proximity to the main road had led to the attractive red brick being covered with a layer of black grime. Since it had been converted into flats in the early 1960s, the cream paintwork on the doors and windows had turned a tawdry brown and in many places had peeled off altogether, revealing the bare woodwork. At first he thought the building was half-empty for the downstairs windows were lined with blackened net curtains but when he pushed open the front door and walked up the stairs to flat 6 he realised he had been wrong in his assessment. Behind the door of the first floor flat reggae music blared out, intermixed with Afro-Caribbean voices.

Flat 6 was at the top of the building and appeared to be a loft conversion. Finding no bell, he rapped loudly on the door, then waited. A middle-aged woman with a tired face, stood on the threshold and eyed him suspiciously.

"Yes?"

He showed his warrant card.

"Detective Constable Thomas. I rang earlier."

"Oh yes. You'd best come in. I can't spare you long. I've got the dinner on."

He walked through a dim hallway lit by a naked bulb, into a small sparsely furnished sitting room. There was a lived-in feel to the room as if the occupant rarely left the premises. The heat in the room was almost unbearable and he noticed that all the windows were firmly shut and appeared to be painted in with thick, white gloss paint which had turned a nicotine brown. Just his luck. No air.

"So you've come about Jack? Is that right?" the woman asked, sitting down in one of the wicker chairs and lighting a cigarette.

"That's right."

"What do you want to ask me? He's been dead three years," she added, as if her observation might make any further discussion entirely worthless.

"I want to ask you about a woman he knew – an Isabelle Le Conte."

For a moment Hazel Slade did not reply but tapped her cigarette agitatedly against the ash tray on the table, sending a fine spray of white ash into the air.

"Did you know this woman?" he asked, producing the photograph from his pocket. She glanced at it casually.

"Yes, I knew her. I met her once – briefly – at one of Jack's showings in the Academy. She was with her husband at the time."

"This was when?"

"I don't remember exactly. 1971 I think. Why? Is it important?"

"It might be. What can you tell me about your husband's relationship with this woman, Mrs Slade?"

"I'd rather you called me Hazel if you don't mind. I don't like to be referred to as Mrs Slade."

"Is that right? And why is that?"

"I've done my time in the marriage stakes, put up with a great deal when Jack was alive. Now I'm independent. I do as I like. And that's how it's going to be from now on. The name Slade isn't mine any more. Only by association."

Thomas placed the photograph back in his jacket.

"What kind of man was Jack Slade?"

"He was a brilliant painter. That's the first thing you need to know. But it's by no means the most important thing. He was also selfish to the core, bigoted and completely promiscuous. I put up with it for twelve years before I left him. He lived for two years after that. Then the cancer killed him."

"Were you living together when he met Isabelle?"

She shook her head.

"We'd separated by then. We'd occasionally meet up – not very often. I always supported his professional work, though. Made an effort to turn up to his exhibitions. That's how I met her you see."

"What did you make of her?"

"Tall, very elegant, intelligent. Just the sort of woman who appealed to Jack. He painted her you know. I've got it here – in the back room. Want to have a look?"

"OK. Thanks."

She stubbed out her cigarette and led the way into a small second bedroom, which clearly served as a makeshift office. The walls were hung with a series of vivid paintings, many of them landscapes applied with thick, heavy strokes of the brush. Among these were two large nudes, one a large, fleshy woman in her sixties, wearing nothing but a large floppy hat, the other was of a tall, voluptuous woman, leaning back on a chaise longue, one leg dangling on the floor, the other raised on a cushion. The face, which was facing forwards, was long and fine-boned with high cheek bones and a broad forehead, framed by dark hair. There was a serenity to her stare which lent the painting an added dimension and the dark drapes which formed the background, gave the piece an unusual intensity.

"You don't know where this was completed, I suppose?" he asked.

"No, I don't. As I said, at that stage we weren't living together. I believe they met at the Academy. Her husband lectured at the university. They used to come over for the summer term. He – the husband – was a lecturer in Fine Art. They might even have known each other way back. I don't rightly know. I never knew the half of it. In those days I used to turn up at his studio in Denmark Street and find he wasn't there. At the time I didn't know he'd be at some other woman's flat or wherever. It went on for years like that. In the end friends of ours used to tell me about his other women. He was good at keeping secrets, you see. God knows how many other women he must have had. She was just part of his collection. Why are you interested in this woman, anyway?"

"She was murdered. We think it was some time in 1972, though we're not absolutely sure about the exact date. We're trying to build up a picture regarding her last movements. So any information you can give us might prove useful. According to her husband, she left France in 1972 in order to live with your husband but what we don't know is how long she was with him before she was murdered. You don't recall seeing them together during the first half of that year, for example?"

She looked thoughtful, then walked back into the living room and began rummaging in a battered box file.

"Diary for '72," she said. "Here we are. This will jog the memory."

She began leafing through the pages.

"He had two exhibitions during the winter and spring of '72," she said. "I went to both of them. No note here of seeing this woman. Unless of course I simply didn't make a note of it.

But I think I would have. That takes us to May, June, July. Let's see. No. I didn't see him then. Not at all."

"Where was he living?"

"As I say he had a flat in Denmark Street. A two-roomed affair, right at the top of the building. His friend, Andrew, had the basement flat."

"Andrew?"

"An artist friend of Jack's. He's still around. They were close friends, drinking companions. God knows, he should be dead. Cirrhosis of the liver I would imagine. He arranged the funeral. Took care of most of the arrangements."

"You don't have an address for him?"

"Andrew Holden? Yes, I do. I'll get it for you. Are we more or less done? I'm hungry and I need to eat."

CHAPTER TEN
STANTON

At 9am the following morning all the windows in No 27 Great George Street had been flung wide open and the office cleaner was putting the finishing touches to the Formica topped tables as Glenister entered, followed by DCs Thomas, Evans and Bottrell. Dr Frances Leadbetter, who had arrived some time earlier, was sitting on the sofa, making copious notes in a small, leather-bound notebook and as her male colleagues entered, she looked up and smiled.

"OK," said Glenister, looking tired and somewhat dishevelled. "I want to be brief this morning. We have a possible lead on the Brandon Hill murder. A lecturer at the Belmont Language School, one Norman Stanton, was reported yesterday by one of the host parents for making indecent advances to one of the students. We checked his name against the CRO register and it appears that in 1970 he was cautioned for indecent exposure to a female student when he was working in a school in Weston-super-Mare. Evans and I will be questioning him later this morning. If we think we have a viable case for the DPP, we'll obtain a search warrant. Bottrell, I want you and Thomas to sort that out this morning and maybe we'll get over there this afternoon and search his flat. His address is – 26 Cotham Lawn Road, Clifton. No real leads on the double murder case as yet.

We've really got to get our fingers out on this one. They're starting to get edgy, our lords and masters.

"We do believe the two victims may have been killed at different times and by different people – which rather complicates matters. Bottrell, Evans, I want you to check out the background again and see what you can dredge up. Check out their associates. Maybe re-interview this Michelle Brown woman. Somebody has to be holding back on this one. DC Thomas has made some progress with the Isabelle Le Conte case. He's interviewed both former husbands. The woman's lover, who her husband claimed his wife had come to Bristol in '72 to visit, is dead, unfortunately, which doesn't make our job any easier. He's interviewed the man's wife – what's her name?"

"Hazel Slade," Thomas put in.

"Hazel Slade – yes – so we're building a picture, albeit slowly – of her last movements. Too early yet to say if there's a definite link between her murder and the more recent case, but we shall know more when we interview Stanton. Frances. You wanted to make some comments about the Brandon Hill murder?"

Frances stood up and smoothed down her skirt before she spoke.

"There are certain common features to the murder of Isabelle Le Conte and Rachael La Mer. Both victims were obviously French and both were strangers to the city. Both women were roughly of the same height and from a similar social class: upper middle class and from moderately wealthy families. From the evidence we have compiled, we can be fairly certain that both were stalked by their murderers. In the case of Rachael La Mer, she appears to have been taken completely by surprise when the attack took place. Both were attacked in quite public places which suggests an element of daring on behalf of their assailants. In the case of Rachael, it's possible that the murderer was a woman – or it could equally be a man of small stature. This we know because of the footprint evidence and the angle of the blows. We can also tell from the severity of the knife wounds and their depth that in both cases the murderer was motivated by extreme anger or hatred – an all-consuming emotion. There are several reasons why this sort of attack can be caused by such rage. Perhaps the perpetrator hates women. possibly one woman in particular. Perhaps the relationship was an abusive one. I would say this is a dangerous loner. Someone playing God. Taking revenge for something."

Glenister looked thoughtful.

"So will he – or she – strike again?"

"In my view, yes. Without doubt. Both killings are the actions of a compulsive, psychopathic personality."

"And a paedophile?"

"I wouldn't think it's likely, no. Neither victim was sexually assaulted. This is a person who lives alone – not in the literal sense, but whose inner world is all consuming. As I mentioned previously, this person is driven by the need to kill, because, through the act of killing, he or she gains an emotional release. That doesn't mean to say that the person will strike over a short period of time. There may be gaps in the pattern of killing during which time the killer will contemplate how the murder will be carried out. The person we're dealing with will have spent a great deal of time and effort preparing each act. He or she lives in an ordered world and is meticulous about details. So this is the kind of person we're looking for, gentlemen, a dangerous psychopath. Hot tempered too I should imagine."

"A deranged killer," observed Glenister.

"In the popular sense, maybe, but in reality most serial killers are not deranged. They are extremely rational—"

"And highly intelligent," Bottrell interjected.

"Quite often yes, John," she replied. "In this case, I believe the murderer may have been confined by his or her abuser – perhaps as a child. The act of taping the victims' mouths would suggest that. She or he may have no criminal record, a fact which makes our task even more challenging. These, then, are the facts of the case as far as I can interpret them."

"Any questions, then?" asked Glenister. "No? Well, thanks, Frances, that was impressive."

Frances gave Glenister a quick glance, as if questioning his patronage but Glenister appeared not to notice anything. As she prepared to leave, Bottrell quickly moved to her side in the doorway.

"You're welcome to come over to the flat."

"When?"

"This evening. That is, if you're not doing anything," he added.

She smiled.

"That would be nice," she said.

Outside, in the car, Bottrell turned to Thomas.

"Dave – can you do me a favour?"

"Depends."

"D'you think you could deal with Michelle Brown on your own this morning? There's something I need to check out."

"Personal, is it? Nothing to do with a certain psychologist, I suppose?"

He grinned.

"Nothing at all to do with that, though I'm touched by your concern. No, it's something else entirely."

"It's OK. I'll handle her. Ring me this afternoon at the office. I'll tell you if I've got anything new."

After leaving Thomas, Bottrell made his way out onto Park Road. He sat for a while behind the plate glass window of Rocco's Coffee House, staring at the traffic and the pigeons, as they swooped above the Wills Memorial Building. Weeks of intensive sun and heat and still no rain. The city was beginning to resemble the inside of an incinerator. The parched lawns surrounding the entrance to the university had turned a grotesque yellow and the pavements were peppered with the remains of chewing gum, takeaways and bird droppings. Surely it must rain soon, he thought.

He finished his coffee and made his way in the direction of the Central Library. Once inside, he made straight for the reference section and the filing cabinets holding the Bristol newspapers on microfiche. He located the reel for the Bristol Daily News for September 1876 and soon found what he was searching for. The headline ran:

Pembroke Road Murder: Trial of Charles Rousseau.

'At the Old Bailey today the trial of the Pembroke Road murderer, Charles Henri Rousseau, began. Charles Rousseau was arrested in July for the wilful murder of a French writer and painter, Francois Ypres. During the trial, the jury heard from the prosecution of how, on the twentieth of July, the body of Francoise Ypres was discovered in a trunk in the attic of a house in Pembroke Road, Bristol, by Mr and Mrs Henry Filby, the new owners of the property. The prosecution alleged that Charles Rousseau had murdered Francoise Ypres in a fit of jealous rage. Francoise Ypres was well known as a minor impressionist painter and hailed from the Montmartre district of Paris. The prosecution told the jury that Charles Rousseau had travelled to England with Francoise Ypres after she had left her husband, a wealthy businessman. Charles Rousseau, a French art dealer, who had contacts with the English art trade, had hoped to open a gallery in Park Street in collaboration with an English artist, Henry Dodman, but the venture never came to fruition...'

Bottrell paused. So her name was Francoise and the number of the property was nowhere mentioned. He couldn't be certain that the body had been found at No 10 Pembroke Road. He left the microfiche and went to the shelves where he found a *Kelly's Street Directory* for 1876, then looked up 10 Pembroke Road. Even then the house was divided into flats, fewer in those days, three in all. In Flat 1 lived a Mr and Mrs Stanmore. Flat 2 had Mr and Mrs Phillimore. And, yes, there it was: Charles Henry Rousseau, but no mention of his mistress. But it was Flat 3. The top flat. The flat with access to the attic...

* * *

"You can use my office, gentlemen," said Ronald Savageri. "I can use the adjoining office. It's no problem."

He began shuffling his papers together, then pressed the intercom on his desk.

"Sally, has Norman Stanton arrived yet? I asked him to come into the school for a meeting."

"Yes. He's just arrived." Sally replied. "Shall I send him in?"

"Give me a moment." Savageri stuffed his remaining papers into a battered black briefcase then ambled to the door.

When Stanton knocked on the principal's door, he had at last got a grip on himself. The fit of nerves which had deprived him of a night's sleep had been assuaged by a quarter of a bottle of whisky which had served as his breakfast.

"Come in," Glenister boomed. Stanton opened the door and was at once confronted by Glenister's steely gaze. Next to him sat DC Evans, head bowed, pen at the ready.

"Sit down, Mr Stanton," said Glenister. His voice was calm but cool. Stanton sat in the leather chair opposite them and crossed his arms and legs defensively, peering at them through his heavy-rimmed glasses.

"Mr Stanton. You know why we've asked to see you?" said Glenister.

"I can guess."

"No. I'd like you to tell us why you think we should want to speak to you," Glenister persisted.

"Because of this business with Rachael La Mer?"

"Yes, but not just that. We understand that one of the host parents, a Reverend Halbett, has made a complaint about your behaviour towards a student, Antoinette Livre."

"Yes, that's correct. However, that was all a misunderstanding."

"And how is that exactly?"

"The young woman in question had made certain advances towards me."

"That's not what she said."

"Maybe, but that's what happened, Inspector, I can assure you."

"She says you invited her to your lodgings…"

"I did. For additional tuition. I frequently do that with students."

"And while she was there you appeared to her in a bath towel and made advances to her."

"I'd had a shower and came out looking for my shirt. I thought she'd left. It was an unfortunate coincidence."

"And the student who made an allegation against you in Weston-super-Mare, was that merely a coincidence too?"

Stanton's face tightened.

"That charge was dropped."

"Nevertheless, an allegation was made against you. And when a charge is made, it's my experience that there's usually some basis in fact for it. What did you do – pay her off?"

Stanton laughed shrilly.

"Really, Inspector, do you think I'd be that indiscreet?"

"Many are," replied Glenister and stared at the round-faced, podgy little man opposite him. He loathed interviewing paedophiles.

"Tell me, Mr Stanton," he said, lowering his voice slightly and leaning forwards.

"Can you give an account of your whereabouts for the evening of July 25th, between 6pm and midnight?"

"I'm not sure Inspector. What day are we talking about?"

"We're talking about Friday last."

Stanton dipped his hand in his jacket pocket and, bringing out a small, leather-bound diary, began to leaf through its pages.

"Let me see, yes, I got an Indian takeaway from the restaurant on Whiteladies Road, then did some marking that evening. A fairly common Friday evening in fact."

"Can anyone vouch for that?"

"Well, I suppose you could ask the restaurant staff. They know me quite well, but apart from them, no, I don't suppose so."

"Rachael La Mer – I believe she was a student of yours?"

"Yes she was."

"And how would you describe her?"

"Very able. Achieved good results, especially in conversational English."

"You got on well with her?"

"Yes."

"And did you invite her to take extra tutorial sessions?"

Stanton pursed his lips in annoyance.

"No I didn't. It wasn't necessary. She didn't need them."

"You're sure about that?"

"Yes, I am."

"Because, as you know, we can interview her classmates and check out your story."

"I have no reason to lie to you."

"Is that so?"

There was an uncomfortable silence.

"What's the name of the restaurant in Whiteladies Road?"

"The Bengal Star."

Evans made a note of it.

"We shall need to search your flat, Mr Stanton. Hope that's not a problem for you?"

"I regard that as an invasion of privacy. I'd rather you didn't."

"Then we shall obtain a search warrant."

"On what grounds?"

"We have sufficient grounds. May I remind you this is a murder enquiry?"

"And I'm a suspect I suppose?"

"You would not be wrong in that assumption. You're not under arrest of course. You are free to go but we may need to interview you again."

Stanton stood up, looking angry.

"I regard this as victimisation."

"Regard it however you want. It makes no odds to me, Mr Stanton. That's all for now. Please close the door behind you as you leave."

Stanton made his way down the corridor, his face white with fury.

"Everything alright, Mr Stanton?" asked Sally as he left. He did not reply.

* * *

DC Dave Thomas parked the car at the end of the cul-de-sac and sat for a moment with the driver's window wound down, looking for his notebook and listening to the sound of a train as it clanked its way slowly through Parson Street railway station. The air was humid and smelt of cooked breakfasts and discarded takeaways. He glanced in the rear view mirror. The street was quiet except for a couple of youths kicking a football about at the far end of the street. So engrossed were they in their game that they hardly noticed him. Both wore the uniform he had come to associate with the youth of the impoverished area: the dreadlocks, black power T-shirts, the hipster trousers and doc martin boots. He wound up the window, then got out and locked the car. Best to be on the safe side.

He made his way past overgrown gardens until he drew level with the front door. It lay slightly ajar. From inside he could hear a baby crying and there was a smell of burning food. He knocked loudly on the paint-peeled door and waited, but there was no reply.

He pushed the door wide, stepped inside and called again, this time louder.

"Michelle Brown?"

Still no answer. He carried on slowly down the hallway, alert, cautious. Something wasn't quite right. He could sense it. Smoke was coming from the kitchen. He opened the door. A pan was alight on the hob. He grabbed a tea towel, wrapped it round the handle and dropped it into the sink, then turned off the gas. The baby's wailing grew louder. It was coming from one of the rooms upstairs. He was about to climb the stairs when he noticed a shape through the crack of the living room door. He was about to enter when he saw the bloody footprint at the entrance. Elongated blood spatters on the wall of the hallway confirmed his worst suspicions.

He took a handkerchief from his pocket and pushed the door open. The body of Michelle Brown lay face down, the dark hair matted with blood. He knelt down, careful to avoid the crimson pool which seeped from beneath her.

The mouth lay open, the teeth broken and bloody, the nose smashed to a pulp. He felt for a pulse in the neck but there was none. The flesh was still slightly warm. He looked at his watch. 11.30am. He made a mental note of the time. He stood up again. Dripped and expirated bloodstains on the textured carpet and on the edge of the skirting board. Impact spatter on the wall by the standard lamp along with a small void, indicating Michelle's attacker had stood over her to deliver his final, lethal blows. He followed the carpet towards the door. A smudged, half print of a left foot. Another smaller smudge of blood on the door handle, possibly a print. On the wall adjacent to the door was a series of low velocity spatter stains with projections, indicating the killer's movement towards the back door, showing where the blood had dripped from his hand and the murder weapon.

Keeping to the edge of the hall carpet, he made his way to the back door and, finding it open, knelt down to examine the handle. Another set of prints, a thumb and forefinger this time, very clearly defined.

In the back garden he looked round for a possible murder weapon but the space was almost bare of debris. He noticed a small garden shed, adjoining a low fence. Beyond it was an alleyway.

He peered over the fence. Another footprint, and on the fence, a fresh splinter where the killer's jacket or trousers had snagged. He picked up a small stick and carefully levered the shed door open. The sunlight streamed in through the opaque window, picking out a rusting lawn mower, a broken broom and two bags of compost. Then he spotted it. On the floor a short piece of lead pipe, one end smeared with blood.

He walked back up the path, entered the back door and again heard the baby. It gave a long sustained wail of sorrow. He was torn between comforting the child and returning to the car. He decided on the latter. He must be quick about it and then secure the murder scene and wait for forensics.

He'd got to the front door when a tall, well-built figure with long dreadlocks appeared making his way up the garden path.

"Who the hell are you?" the man challenged him.

"Police. Who are you?"

"Ashley Geddings. I live here. Where's Michelle? What's happened?" he demanded, staring up towards the bedroom window, listening to the wail of the child.

"I'm sorry, sir, but I must ask you to stay with me. Just for a short while. You can't go inside yet, I'm afraid."

"What do you mean? What's happened?" he shouted.

"Are you a relative?"

"Boyfriend. What's happened to Michelle?" he insisted.

Thomas placed a restraining hand on his shoulder.

"I'm afraid she's been attacked. I'm about to phone the emergency services."

Geddings pushed past him into the house, shouting her name.

"Sir!" he shouted.

But he knew it was useless to try to stop him. He walked back briskly to the car and began to phone in the details of the incident on the radio. When he returned he found Geddings sitting in the porch, cradling the baby. He was rocking backwards and forwards. When Thomas spoke to him he didn't reply but uttered a single low moan, tears streaming down his face. There was a prolonged silence. A woman walked by on the pavement and paused to stare at them, then moved on, humming to herself.

"The bastard. The bastard." Geddings growled, his face grim.

CHAPTER ELEVEN
GHOSTS

She looked at her watch. 9.15am. Time to look at her collection. Taking the small Yale key from her purse, she inserted it into the lock of the walk-in cupboard and opened the door. It was quiet in the house. The people above her had left for work earlier that morning and her husband had left fifteen minutes ago. She always waited, just to be safe, for on one occasion he had returned, having forgotten his briefcase and had taken her by surprise. She had only just heard in time and managed to leave the cupboard, locking the door behind her. It had been a close shave and one she didn't care to repeat.

Jack had never been curious about the cupboard and if he had, he had learnt to suppress his curiosity. He had mentioned it only once to her and she had told him that it wasn't useable, that the previous occupants had told her that it was far too small and that there was no key to gain entry. Her tone of voice was one he had become familiar with. Sharp, authoritative and never to be questioned. He had taken her word for it.

Jack invariably took her word for it. He was not very bright and in many ways it suited her. She had met him at a Who concert at the Corn Exchange three years ago. She didn't normally go to such things but on this occasion she had been persuaded by someone at work who had not wanted to go alone. She had been flattered really. She had few, if any, friends.

Jack was a tall, well-built youth with a Beatle haircut and a gauche manner. He had had little experience with women and soon admitted to her that he was still a virgin. He was so inexperienced that she had had to initiate him. Her early rape had influenced her greatly. The brutal act had served to detach her from the emotional act of love. She had felt nothing but the need to be satisfied. They had sex frequently. Her appetite was large and he was always obedient. He would always thank her afterwards, since it was the only close contact that they had and his childlike need for physical contact was very strong. It reinforced her role as the initiator and the controller.

He was strong and well-endowed and she liked the feel of his firm legs and body, rising and falling above her as she whispered instructions to him. But even at the height of her climax she was still in control, her mind cold and calculating. Often she would take him from above and ride him roughly like some toy and her orgasms were all the more satisfying.

In the first year of their marriage Jack told her he was keen to have children. She expressed limited interest in the subject but nevertheless went along with the idea, scheduling their sessions together when she was at her most fertile. Perhaps it would be good for her, she thought, another doll to control and play with. Within three months she found she was pregnant but when her GP broke the news, she was far from happy about it. Reality began to sink in. From that point onwards she stopped the sex. Jack was devastated and withdrew into himself. For weeks they didn't speak and even ate at separate times. She insisted on sleeping alone and was glad of the big bed and the space to indulge her own thoughts without interruption.

146

Although Jack had satisfied her bodily needs, their conversations were very limited. He had not flourished at school. His dullness had frustrated his parents and teachers. The only subject that he had had any success in, was maths. It required little imagination – just facts. At the age of sixteen he had left school and gone straight into the insurance business. He read little, apart from the *Daily Mirror*, and they spent most of their evenings together watching TV. Sometimes he would be required to service her when she felt the need, whatever he was doing. He became part of her collection. In time, she thought she would leave him altogether.

She hated that pregnancy. She was violently sick on a regular basis and was ill at ease with this thing that had started to invade her body. It had taken control; every waking moment of her life was affected. She felt vulnerable for the first time since her youth.

She had conceived once before, immediately after the rape, but had aborted early in the pregnancy after taking some quinine tablets that her one friend at school had acquired for her. The bitter taste had made her ill and she had vowed never to use them again. She had managed to keep the entire episode a secret from her mother. If she had found out, she might never have survived the beatings.

Week by week she grew fatter and more sluggish. Matters were not helped by the hot summer weather. Through the latter stage of her pregnancy she continued to drink and smoke heavily, ignoring her GP's advice. It was as if she had a death wish, not for herself but for the child inside her.

Then, one day in late July, she had been making her way down the escalator in the city centre when she slipped and fell. Two shoppers helped her to her feet but she was severely shaken and eventually got a taxi back to the flat, having refused offers to take her to the hospital so that she could be checked out. She made herself a cup of tea, then sat on the sofa, a sharp pain shooting through her abdomen. The pain didn't go away. In fact it got worse. In desperation she picked up the phone and rang the emergency services. The ambulance arrived some twenty minutes later, by which time she knew her labour had begun.

She was admitted to the maternity ward of the Infirmary but from the moment the double doors swung shut behind her she knew that the child was no longer moving. It took two hours of pain and torment before she was rid of the thing. The nurse wrapped the baby in a towel and spoke to her in a low, apologetic voice. There was nothing they could have done. The child had been stillborn.

Jack arrived at the hospital an hour later, distraught. She felt nothing but relief at what had happened. A great sense of calm enveloped her, no longer was her life out of control. Her body was hers once more.

"We can try again," Jack had told her. "It's not the end of the world."

But for her, it was the end. She would have none of it and she told him so. After that, their physical relationship began to diminish. She used him very occasionally to satisfy her need but when the deed was done she would push him off her and cover her body with the sheet, choosing not to speak to him. She would find another way to satisfy her needs.

Some months later she bought a pram. It was an old fashioned model with large wheels and a high hood. She had seen it in a second-hand shop and had chosen it deliberately because of its large size. When Jack came home from work that evening he saw it standing in the hall outside the flat and beamed at her.

"You've changed your mind!" he said, his voice exultant.

"We'll have to wait." she said in a stern voice. "This is just in case."

Jack bounced into the flat like a child. She smiled to herself. The pill would put a stop to that nonsense.

And that was how it had begun. Each day, shortly after nine, she would open the walk-in cupboard, switch on the small lamp and sit staring at her collection, each one dressed immaculately in its handmade skirt and blouse. Then she would take each one in turn and comb its hair before replacing it and readjusting its pose. Some would be kneeling, some standing, others lying as if asleep. After some while she would choose one, her companion for the day, her silent friend. Briefly addressing it, she would place the doll in the large pram so that only the face was visible to her, then wheel the pram from the flat hallway out onto the street towards the park. Here she would sit, listening to the sounds of the birds, watching the passersby as they paused to feed the ducks on the wide pond. For two hours she would sit there, rocking the pram gently, attracting smiles from young mothers as they passed with their pushchairs. But if they came too close she would glare at them or quickly move on to another part of the park until they had disappeared. Beneath the large hood the diminutive figure was almost invisible. Sitting there on the bench by the pond with the pram next to her and the small, stiff, silent, obedient figure wrapped in its yellow blanket, she felt unassailable, in control.

She glanced again at her watch. 9.30am. Time for that walk. She reached for the Victorian china doll with the large eyes and crinoline skirt. Her name was Samantha and today she was the chosen one. She straightened and brushed her hair, then laid her gently in the pram, tucking the yellow blanket in around her. Then, going back to the cupboard and reaching up to the shelf, she brought out the dark lock of hair and placed the small trophy inside the pram, next to the long bladed knife with the black handle which was also her constant companion. It was time to leave.

* * *

Walker was leaning over the body of Michelle Brown when Glenister and Leadbetter arrived. In his white forensic suit and latex gloves he looked like some strange alien hovering over his prey. So preoccupied was he that he barely noticed the arrival of his two colleagues, moving from side to side of the corpse, almost appearing to caress his subject, occasionally stopping to make whispered observations into his portable tape recorder. After some while he slowly stood up, the plastic suit creaking, wiping the perspiration from his forehead.

"Well, Doug?" enquired Glenister.

"Just mind where you're treading will you?" he replied sharply. "You should both be wearing slip-ons."

"Sorry," said Glenister, glancing down at his feet. "So we should."

"Too late now," grumbled Walker. "This is an almighty mess, anyhow. Complicated scenes of crime I can well do without."

Glenister knelt down and stared at the crumpled form of Michelle Brown. The warm air smelt of cigarettes and stale blood.

"How did she die? Blunt object?" he asked.

"Correct. Quite a savage attack which started in the hallway. As far as I can make out she let in her attacker. No sign of forced entry, so she probably knew him. Defensive blows to the hands and forearms. Several abrasions and contusions. There's also a crush fracture on the left forearm. She put up quite

150

a fight, mind. He pursued her into here, hitting her in the face as she stood by the wall. Look here, you see this expiration spatter? That's where she went down. The final, lethal blow was delivered from behind. Shattered part of the cranium. You can see where he stood to do it."

Glenister looked round the room.

"What about these footprints?"

"Yes, what a mess! Like a herd of elephants has been through here. Two sets of footprints. I take it DC Thomas has filled you in on the details?"

"No, not yet. Where is he?"

"Left when I arrived. Something about getting a search warrant. No idea what for."

Glenister ground his teeth irritably.

"He should be here. He should not have left. What did he tell you?"

Walker removed his surgical gloves and blew his nose loudly on a crisp white handkerchief.

"He arrived here at 11.30 this morning. He was about to phone the incident through when the boyfriend turned up. He tried to prevent him from gaining entry but he pushed past him. Buggered up my crime scene in other words."

Glenister shook his head despairingly.

"So one set of footprints belongs to the boyfriend, is that it?"

"Most likely, yes."

"What about fingerprints?"

"Two sets of prints on the door handle. And a further print on the murder weapon, a piece of lead pipe which Thomas found in the shed out the back. I've bagged it."

"So what's the boyfriend's story?"

"Says he'd popped out to the betting shop, then gone to his flat to collect his mail. Gone about twenty minutes."

"Did Thomas notice any sign of blood staining on his clothes?"

Walker took a long thermometer from his case and began turning the body over, preparing to insert it. Glenister averted his gaze. Sometimes the details of forensic investigation were quite repulsive to him.

"He was wearing a clean T-shirt and freshly ironed trousers, according to Thomas."

"Maybe he murdered her, then went back home and changed."

"Maybe. It's possible."

"Where is this boyfriend?"

"Sitting in the squad car with WPC Swinton. There's also a baby in there, so you might want to talk to him in your own car."

"Have social services been contacted yet?" asked Frances, who had been silent up until now, quietly absorbing the information.

"I believe WPC Swinton has been on to them," Walker replied. "Not my concern, I'm afraid. Ah, I think that's my team arriving. Excuse me, will you?"

Two men had appeared in the doorway, both in the customary white plastic suits and both clutching small metal cases.

"Come in, gentlemen. There's plenty of fodder for you."

Glenister groaned and grimaced at Leadbetter. She shook her head wearily.

Ashley Geddings was sitting in the front of the police car, his head in his hands, his long dark dreadlocks splayed out behind him. From the back of the car came the harsh cry of Michelle Brown's baby. WPC Swinton was cradling it in her arms, rocking it gently, trying to calm the child. Glenister opened the car door and looked in.

"Ashley Geddings? I'm DCI Glenister and this is my colleague, Dr Leadbetter. We'd like a word, please. My car, if you wouldn't mind."

Geddings wiped the tears from his face and followed them down the road. Glenister offered him a cigarette.

"Perhaps you'd like to tell us what happened here," he said in a matter of fact tone.

"I'd been out to the bookies. Then back to my flat to change and collect my post. When I got back here—"

"What time was that?"

"Just before twelve I think. I got back here and found this guy on the doorstep."

"DC Thomas."

"Yes. Him. I asked him what's up but he don't tell me nothing. Says I can't go inside. I can hear the baby crying upstairs so I pushed past him. Then I found her, lying there."

"OK. We shall need your shoes."

"Why?"

"Because you've disturbed a crime scene. You really should have listened to DC Thomas. Your barging in complicates matters. Show me your shoes. As I thought. There's blood on your left shoe. We shall also need the clothes you were wearing when you left the house."

"What for?"

"To eliminate you from our enquiries of course. It's a matter of procedure. Where do you live?"

"Thackeray Street. Number 12."

"OK. Take these shoes off and give them to Dr Leadbetter here. Have you got an evidence bag?" he said, turning to Frances.

"I'll get one."

"What about the child?" asked Geddings.

"It's OK. Social Services will take care of her for now. You wait here with me, then we'll take you round to your flat."

Geddings looked agitated.

"What's on your mind?" Glenister asked him.

"I know who done this," he said.

"Done what?"

"Killed Michelle. I know who killed her!"

"And who killed her, Ashley?"

"Roy N'como."

"And why would he kill Michelle?"

"Because she gave his name to you people. She should never have done that."

"Is that right?"

"Yeah, that's right."

"And why would he want to silence her?"

"Because it was N'como who killed Kevin and Michael. And she knew it."

"Why would he kill them? For what possible reason?"

"Because they killed his son."

"Is that a fact?"

"It's true. They were out joyriding. They'd taken a good deal of shit. Kevin was driving. They turned a corner in Wendron Street and the boy was crossing the road. Kevin didn't see him. He was high, man. The car went straight into him, killed him. There were two witnesses. Friends of Nathaniel – that was N'como's son. Kevin paid them to keep quiet about the matter. But N'como found out about it anyway. I'm telling you, he killed them."

"You're prepared to make a statement?"

He nodded.

"I'll make a statement."

"Alright then. We'll take you to your flat, then you can come down to the station and we'll do that."

"What about the child?"

"We'll sort that out. First things first. Now. Let's have those shoes, shall we?"

* * *

Cotham Lawn Road lay in the prosperous hinterland of Redland. It had been constructed for wealthy merchants in the mid-Victorian period and its houses were built with solid limestone blocks. Tall Palladian columns dominated the fronts of these villas. Each one lay back from the road and was surrounded by high privet hedges and large hydrangea bushes. Several of the houses had conservatories built on to their fronts and one or two had loft conversions, which looked totally incongruous and broke the line of the roof tops.

It was in the rooftop studio of No 26 that Norman Stanton lived. He had been here a number of years now and, having purchased the flat for a pittance, had converted it according to his needs. The lounge, where he spent much of his time alone, was furnished with wall to wall bookcases. These housed his collection of European erotica. For Norman Stanton was a collector of rare editions and over the last twenty years had accumulated an impressive collection of Victorian pornography. The second bedroom housed an equally bizarre array of objects – manacles, chains, an assortment of whips and various instruments of bondage. This room he kept locked, especially when conducting his unofficial tutorials with female students. It was his refuge, his inner sanctum. Every week he would invite Sarah, a local prostitute, to this room where Norman would submit himself to a variety of degrading acts under the severe eye of his dominatrix. In this way he kept a check on his libido. In Norman's words, 'the beast sleeps with one eye open'.

Norman's other passion was centred upon his female students. Young, fresh faced and virginal, they were a constant source of temptation to Norman and he was always intoxicated by their presence. He had twice erred from the 'paths of righteousness' as he called it, and on both occasions he had regretted his actions. The most recent example, involving his incident with Antoinette, was something he had come to regret, especially since it now threatened to undermine his position at the language school.

It therefore came as something of a shock to him when the doorbell rang at lunch time and he found two plain clothes police officers on his doorstep. He had just made himself a sandwich and was settling down to listen to the new recording of Beethoven's Emperor Concerto, when they arrived. Carefully folding the new edition of 'Young Hot Girls' and placing it back inside the plain brown bag, he tucked it into his brief case, then answered the door.

DCs Bottrell and Thomas held out their warrant cards.

"Norman Stanton? Police. We have a warrant to search these premises."

* * *

Ronald Savageri levered his ample form from the executive office chair and opened the door. Sally Acre entered, holding a silver tray with a large coffee pot and four cups.

"Thank you, Sally. Would you please intercept my calls for the next hour? And no interruptions please."

"Very well, principal."

Removing his large cotton jacket, Savageri placed it over the back of his chair and eased himself back into the seat. Opposite him sat a middle-aged man with greying hair, wearing a faded sports jacket with patched sleeves. Next to him sat his wife, Cynthia, a tall woman half his age. Her worn, lined face belied her age. Her face bore a permanent scowl and the lines had been etched into her face like furrows of bark on an oak tree. Cynthia was the Reverend Halbett's amanuensis, his cook, secretary and severest critic. She did not tolerate his weaknesses and showed scant regard for his appalling memory. She had married beneath her station and was constantly aghast at the size of her husband's stipend and did her best to remind him of it. She was dressed in a severe black pinstriped suit, the lines hard and clinical and she had scraped her thin hair back from her face in a tight bun.

It had been Cynthia's idea to accommodate French students to 'augment our credit' as she called it. Digby Halbett had meekly obliged, though privately he had not been looking forward to having his privacy intruded upon. As it turned out, however, Antoinette was a delightful and intelligent girl who spoke constantly in English, much to his relief, and with whom he had struck up an immediate rapport.

When Antoinette had returned home from her 'extra' tutorial session with Stanton, and told them about the bathrobe incident, Cynthia had been outraged. Digby had sat at the dining room table looking shocked but saying nothing. He was not completely surprised by what had happened. Years back, when he had been a curate in Birmingham, he had walked into the vestry to find the vicar of All Saints taking advantage of a small choirboy. It had taken some persuasion for him to remain silent on the matter but had served as a salutary reminder that such incidents were not rare in his calling.

Next to Digby Halbett sat Antoinette. A tall girl with high cheekbones and full lips, she sat erect, folding her long legs, her manicured hands resting on her lap. She was dressed in a tight fitting, classic black suit. Her dark, lustrous hair was cut close to the neck in a pageboy style and she wore expensive silver jewellery. She was her father's daughter: aspirational, articulate, self confident and aware of her beauty.

"The reason we are here," began Cynthia in her usual self-assured manner, "is to determine what you and the governors intend to do about Mr Stanton."

Savageri steepled his hands and attempted to look unphased by the request.

"I can assure you, Mrs Halbett, that the matter is being dealt with."

"In what way exactly?"

"Mr Stanton has been interviewed by the police about the matter."

"And the private tutorials?"

"And the tutorials. I have also suspended Mr Stanton on full pay, pending a proper enquiry into the matter."

"Conducted by whom?"

"Conducted by me, Mrs Halbett. That's partly why I was eager to meet with you both and Antoinette today. I need to ask Antoinette some questions."

"You realise that if this appalling little man is ever reinstated here, we shall withdraw our support as host parents? We shall also take the matter to the papers."

"That will not be necessary, I can assure you. The matter is quite safe in my hands. Antoinette, I need to know more about Mr Stanton and how the incident occurred. Perhaps you could go over the details?"

Antoinette uncrossed her legs, smoothed the creases from her skirt, then stared unblinkingly at Savageri rather like a lizard watching a fly.

"Very well," she replied, in an almost perfect English accent. "What do you wish to know?"

"Well, for a start, how long had these tutorials been going on?"

"I had five or six I think. Mr Stanton offered extra lessons to those of us who needed extra help, some of the girls had poor English. Others, like myself, were at the advanced stage."

"And during the other sessions, did Mr Stanton ever do anything improper or make inappropriate suggestions to you?"

"No, certainly he didn't. He is a good teacher. He was very encouraging to all of us. He offered to take my photograph."

"Oh yes? What did that entail?"

"He was a photographer. He showed me some of his work. He had some black and white pictures he had taken. They were very good."

"And you had your photograph taken?"

"Why yes. I thought it would be a nice memory of my visit to England – something I could take home to France."

"And other girls – they had their photographs taken too, did they?"

"Yes, he showed me them. He told me he had been a – professional – is that the word? He had worked with the best models in London. That's what I want to be when I have finished my studies – a model. Or maybe an actress."

"I see. And when you sat for these photographic sessions – did he ever ask you to take your clothes off?"

"He said he could take some of me in my bikini if I liked, but I said no."

There was a pause as Savageri made a note on his pad. Cynthia was staring at him with a mixture of determination and outrage. Digby held his head in his hands.

"When Mr Stanton appeared to you in the bathrobe, how exactly did this happen?" he asked.

"We had finished the tutorial. He had asked me if I wanted a fruit juice. He went into the kitchen and poured the juice and then he came back with it. I'd taken my jacket off because it was very hot in there. He asked me if I wanted to take a shower. I thought this was not right so I said no. He said he would not be a moment, he had something he wanted me to see. So I waited. He came out of his bedroom wearing his bathrobe. He began to flatter me. Said I looked beautiful... many things I was not happy with. When I looked down at his bathrobe and saw what he was – how he was – you know, what he is up to, what is happening to him. I became afraid. When he came close and tried to kiss me – well that's when I hit him. Hard."

There was an embarrassed silence. Antoinette bowed her head in shame.

Savageri gave a sigh of resignation.

"Yes, Antoinette. Thank you. I think I've got the picture."

CHAPTER TWELVE
QUESTIONS

Doug Walker unzipped the body bag and waited. For a moment there was silence, then Jean Le Conte put a hand to his mouth as if to smother his grief. He nodded.

"Is this your wife, Isabelle?"

"I am sure. That's her coat. And the ring. That's her wedding ring. Yes, it's Isabelle."

Walker zipped the bag up, then pushed the trolley back into the metal receptacle.

"Perhaps you'd like to take Mr Le Conte back into the reception area, Dave," he suggested.

Thomas escorted his visitor through the double doors into a small waiting area equipped with a low sofa and two chairs.

"Coffee or tea?" he asked.

"Coffee would be good."

When he returned bearing a tray with two cups of black coffee, Le Conte looked more composed. He drank the coffee straight down, then reached into his jacket pocket for a packet of cigarettes.

"Can I smoke in here?" he asked.

"We're not supposed to, but, under the circumstances," replied Thomas, offering him a lighter.

"I can't believe it's her," he said, inhaling deeply. "That thing in there isn't Isabelle. It's just a shell. If it hadn't been for her mac and the ring…"

"The worst is over now," Thomas replied. "It's always the most difficult part."

"I thought she was still alive, you know. Just didn't want to have anything more to do with us. It took me a while to accept it. But now, knowing… it is somehow much worse."

Le Conte offered him a cigarette.

"I need to ask you about Isabelle." said Thomas.

"Oui?"

"After I left you, I went to see Henri Fleur in Trouville. He told me Isabelle had a child some while before she married him."

"Yes, she told me about that. What of it?" Le Conte shrugged.

"How old was she when this happened?"

"About sixteen I think. When she became pregnant. She was called Isabelle Giscard then. She lived in Honfleur. Her father was a fisherman, and her mother – she was very pious? Religious, I think. They both were. When she told them they asked the priest what they should do. He said to have the baby adopted… given to someone else, *n'est ce pas*? They lived in a large house on the edge of the town. Madame Giscard rented her rooms to foreign tourists. There was a couple who used to visit every year. They had no children. Every summer they came. They were called – ah – let me see."

Le Conte paused, trying to remember the name of the couple. Thomas shifted, impatiently.

"The name was 'Stuart' I think. The man was from Scotland. Michael – I think his name was Michael. From the east side of Scotland. The wife was an artiste. Stephanie. M Giscard thought she was odd. Very fiery, nervous I think. The Giscards had talked to them about the child. Isabelle was very sad at the thought of giving her child away. They took the child – but I do not know if it was done properly. There are rules about these things. But they took the child with them anyway. Came back with the child a few years after that."

"Can you remember the child's name?"

"It was a little girl. Let me see. Christina? Non... Catherine? Ah. What was it? Carrie. Yes! That was it. They called her Carrie."

"She didn't visit her daughter when you came to England, then?"

"Non. I think the family had moved by then. She did write a few times but she got no reply. Poor Isabelle. She always thought about Carrie, I think. She felt very bad about it. Why, you don't think that was why she came to England? That it was not Slade she came to find?"

"I'm not sure what to believe, to be honest, but it's something I think we should look into."

* * *

DCI Glenister re-entered the interview room, holding two cups of instant coffee. He gave one to Bottrell, then sat at the table and reached for his cigarettes. As the smoke filled the small room, Norman Stanton grimaced, then coughed.

"Is this a problem for you, Stanton?" he asked sarcastically.

"I suffer from asthma. I normally have a nebuliser but I didn't have time to collect it before you people..." His voice trailed off, as if he could not bring himself to refer to the details of his arrest. He had still not come to terms with the event. He had been led from the flat, watched by the elderly occupant of Flat 2, who stood open-mouthed at her front door, her face a

163

mask of indignation mixed with curiosity. After all, Cotham Lawn Road was part of a respectable neighbourhood. Mrs Bentine had often seen young girls going into the apartment and had feared the worse about the activities of her neighbour.

Glenister took a drag from his cigarette, then stubbed it out. The windowless room was airless and claustrophobic. In the fluorescent lighting Stanton looked pale and drawn.

"Let's talk about Rachael La Mer, shall we?" he said, switching on the tape.

"Wednesday August 3rd. 3pm. DCI Glenister and DC Bottrell interviewing Norman Stanton," said Bottrell.

"Rachael La Mer was one of your students. In your statement to us you told us that on Friday July 25th you visited the Bengal Star on Whiteladies Road and ordered a takeaway meal. This was some time after 6pm. That's correct, is it?"

"That's right – yes."

"Well, we had your story checked out with the restaurant staff. Nobody remembers you ordering a takeaway. How do you account for that?"

"I don't understand it. I was there. I can even remember what I ordered."

"You paid in cash I take it?"

"Of course."

"So you can't actually prove that you were there, can you?"

"I suppose not in that case."

"We also checked with some of the female students. Helene Pickard, Rachael's friend, says that Rachael spoke about having had tutorials with you."

"No, that's not correct. She'd asked me about having extra sessions but we never got round to it. I had a waiting list."

"So you were popular with the female students, then?"

"I like to think so."

"When we searched your flat we found some interesting material, as you know."

Bottrell produced a large evidence bag and, opening it, spread out on the table a selection of magazines with lurid titles. 'Hot Girls', 'Young Virgins' and 'Girls Only'.

"This was part of your collection, Norman. For the sake of the tape I'm showing the suspect a number of pornographic magazines. Do you want to tell us about your sexual feelings towards your female students?"

"How dare you! I've always acted correctly towards them."

"That isn't true of Antoinette Livre, though, is it?"

"That was a misunderstanding. I already told you."

"And the girl in Weston-super-Mare? I suppose that was all a misunderstanding too, was it?"

"Look. You have absolutely nothing on me. I've not got a criminal record. I haven't committed an offence. I've never interfered with any female student. It would be more than my job's worth. I told Savageri that. I told him! He had no right to suspend me! I shall appeal against it, you can be sure of that. The whole thing's preposterous. You don't know these girls, Inspector. They can be very precocious, very forward. And they can be very deceitful. You have to watch your back with them."

"I would suggest that the only person being deceitful is yourself, Norman. You were obsessed with Rachael La Mer. Why don't you admit it? You'd asked her to attend one of your tutorials but she refused, didn't she? So on the Friday evening you waited by the quayside and when she got up to leave, you followed her at a discreet distance. You followed her up Brandon Hill and waited until the coast was clear. You got her into the bushes and tried to force yourself on her but when she wasn't having any of it, you stuck a knife in her. Isn't that right?"

Glenister was standing now, leaning forward and shouting at Stanton. Stanton was looking up at Glenister's broad frame, clearly intimidated.

"John, step out for a few minutes, will you?" he said, his voice cold and measured. "I need to speak to Mr Stanton on his own for a while."

Bottrell hesitated, then reluctantly got up to go. He knew what Glenister's intentions were. Stanton's eyes betrayed his fear. Bottrell looked away and left the room, shutting the door firmly behind him, then listened. He could hear Glenister's voice, shouting, accusing, demanding. He heard a bang as a chair was overturned, then a silence, followed by a low whimper. His hand hovered over the door handle, then, thinking better of it, he walked back down the corridor to the coffee machine.

* * *

It was six o'clock. By now the heat of the day had diminished slightly and a breeze wafted in through the large Victorian windows of the language school. She finished hoovering the thick pile carpet, collected up the spare coffee cups and then deposited them in a black bin liner. She began spraying the tables, then spread her duster over the surface and began polishing with long, even strokes, until the surface gleamed. When she had finished she went into the girls' toilets where she bleached the pans, then squirted cleaner into the washbasins and cleaned them with a soft sponge. She found these ritual cleansing sessions strangely satisfying. She was the only person in the school. It was all hers – the classrooms, the cloakrooms, the offices. Nothing interfered with her routine.

When she had finished, she went back into the main corridor and walked past each of the classrooms, checking to see that they were empty, placing the plastic chairs onto the tables. She remembered having to do this when she was young, only then the desks and chairs were wooden, solid and reliable. She positioned each chair correctly, so that they formed a series of straight lines. She enjoyed looking at the rows of chairs. Their uniformity pleased her.

Pushing her trolley along the corridor, she paused, then opened the door to Savageri's office. She tidied the papers on his desk, polishing the surface vigorously and removed the half-full cup of coffee. Then she began to search through the drawers. In the third drawer, in a file marked 'Entrance list: 1976' she found what she was looking for: a typed list of students names complete with dates of birth and the addresses of their host parents. She switched on the photocopier, waited for it to warm up, carefully peering out into the corridor to make sure she was alone, then made a copy of the document, replacing the original in the desk drawer. Then, switching off the machine and the light, she shut the door behind her.

* * *

Bottrell had just opened the oven to examine the progress of the aubergine casserole when the doorbell rang. Discarding the oven gloves, he walked into the hallway and opened the door. Frances stood there.

"Not late am I?"

"No. Not at all. It's great to see you. Enter at your peril," he joked.

They ate slowly, enjoying both the food and each other's company.

"That was good!" said Frances, savouring the last of her wine. She felt full, relaxed and happy. They sat together on the sofa, listening to the Stones' *Brown Sugar* LP, Bottrell stroking her hair gently.

"You heard about Stanton, I take it?"

"Yes, Glenister told me. He was full of it."

"He forced a confession out of him. Frightened the shit out of him."

Frances groaned.

"I told him Stanton shouldn't even be in the frame. He's got the wrong person. He's just a run of the mill sex pervert. He's not a psychopath. Glenister isn't prepared to listen. Like a bloody bull in a china shop. I don't know why he bothers to consult me."

Bottrell sat up and poured them both a brandy.

"The person we're looking for may not even be a man," she continued. "I've told him already. The murderer is someone who's been severely humiliated, probably in childhood. He or she is attempting to come to terms with that humiliation, to take control of it. It's an act of revenge, and a way of seeking catharsis from the suffering, I'm sure of it. There's no sexual element in the murders. Why can't he get that into his thick head for Christ's sake?"

Frances voice had risen with frustration. The wine and brandy had released her anger and he took her hand.

"Hey! Calm down! He's not worth it. He always was pig-headed. He'll find out the hard way that he's got the wrong man. You'll see."

Frances relaxed and leant against him for a moment.

"I'm sorry to get so worked up but the combination of the drink and the heat and Glenister – well they got to me. But anyway, did you get anywhere with your Victorian murder case, by the way?"

He glanced at her hair as it shone in the lamplight. Her body smelled of lavender and her closeness aroused him. He pulled himself together. He mustn't spoil this relationship.

"Yes. I found out quite a bit as a matter of fact."

"Oh really?

"The murdered woman was a painter called Francoise Ypres."

She smiled.

"Ah. That's my name. In French."

"Yes, so it is." replied Bottrell. "She had been murdered by her lover, Charles Rousseau."

"Not *the* Charles Rousseau?"

"Hardly! Anyway at the trial Rousseau confessed to having murdered her after a quarrel. He then put her body in a trunk and stored it in the attic."

"In this house?"

"Yes. It didn't mention the house number in the newspaper account of the trial but I found Rousseau's name in the street directory for 1876. There was no mention of her name but the two of them must have occupied the top flat – flat 3 as it was in those days. The flat was much bigger then and would have included Anne Marie's flat – the flat next door. God knows what Rousseau thought he was going to do with the body. He'd have had to get rid of it at some point. I guess that's why he fled back to France."

"It would explain the feelings you've both had."

"Exactly."

Frances finished her brandy.

"You know John – I think we should have a work free evening, don't you? Next time maybe? I want to get to know you, what you feel, how you think. What do you say? Or am I overstepping the mark?"

Bottrell smiled down at her.

"I think that's the best thing I've heard for a long time. I thought you'd never ask."

He kissed her gently, tasting her lips, savouring the intimacy and the flush of desire he could no longer hide.

Frances pulled away.

"Come on," she said. "It's late and I'm taking you to bed."

They made love, tentatively at first, exploring each other's bodies with growing excitement. For the first time Bottrell found himself swept up in the passion and emotion of the night. Their lovemaking had released a part of himself he had never really acknowledged and the shared climax surprised them both with its intensity. Finally, overcome by exhaustion, Bottrell fell into a profound sleep.

He must have woken with a start sometime in the early morning to find Frances lying across him, her arm extended across his chest. He didn't like to wake her, so he closed his eyes and tried to recall the dream that had woken him.

Much of it was confused and there were gaps but he remembered being in the flat, although much was different. There were gas lamps in brackets on the living room wall and dark, oak chairs either side of a long, Jacobean table. There were heavy velvet curtains at the window and the frames were painted in a dark brown varnish. A large Indian rug covered the pine boards and there was the wide fireplace, much as it was in his own time, only now a real fire burned there. He appeared to be sitting on a high stool and was holding a palette in his left hand, whilst in his right was a paint brush.

Opposite him, lying back on a chaise longue was a young woman with dark hair. There was something Mediterranean

170

about her, he thought. Dark, glossy, curly hair framed a long face. The face itself was aquiline, the eyes sharp and striking, the skin smooth and sallow. One hand rested behind her head, which was raised from the velvet cushion a little, a smile hovering about her lips. Her breasts were full, the nipples erect, the aureoles wide and dark. One leg was raised, the other rested on the floor giving her an almost wanton look. The whole thing was like an evocation of a classical painting. Perhaps a Rembrandt.

The scene began to shift now. The woman was standing with her back to the window.

They appeared to be in the living room. It was night and the room was cloaked in darkness, save for the reflected light from a small gas lamp. She was wearing a long oriental dressing gown which lay open revealing her breasts. He moved forward as if to embrace her but she raised her hand and clutched his, forcing him away. She was speaking to him, her face contorted with emotion, but he could not hear the words. She backed away from him, her long dark hair swirling about her shoulders. She was pointing to something in the garden beyond. He stood next to her at the window and looked down. A figure stood by the bushes. Tall and pale in the moonlight, she pointed back towards the house. Then the moon was lost behind a cloud and the garden was plunged into darkness.

The scene shifted once again. He was alone in the room now, his head resting on the long table. His senses were befuddled as if he had been drinking heavily. He staggered to his feet, then went into the kitchen to get himself a glass of water. When he reached the door to the living room he turned back. She was lying back on the chaise longue. Her dressing gown was open at the chest, her throat had been slashed and her arms splashed crimson with blood. He remembered then what he had done. He went to the kitchen sink and picked up the carving knife. He knew what he had to do. There was a large pine seaman's chest which stood in the corner of the living room. He gripped the knife, then went to the chest and opened the lid, removing the books and bric-a-brac. He would have to shift the chest himself. It would be difficult since it was extremely heavy. He would have to construct some sort of pulley to winch the chest up into the loft. It would be tricky but he had to do something. Then he must leave the flat. Return to France.

The scene began to dissolve. He was looking into a large cupboard. From the shadows he could see the outline of a woman's body and hear a low moaning as if the woman had been gagged. There were other things in the room too, shapes of small figures, toys, books and papers. The figure of the woman shifted, raised her hands. They appeared to be bound with tape. As his eyes grew accustomed to the darkness he saw her bloody face and clothes. The woman's face was somehow familiar to him...

Frances shifted her arm from his chest, then woke suddenly with a start.

"Listen," she said. "Did you hear that?"

"Hear what?"

"The sound of a woman moaning?"

"I can't hear anything. No, nothing."

He looked at the moonlight coming in through the window. The curtains swayed in the breeze.

"It must have been the wind," he said. "Go back to sleep."

But as Frances snuggled down beside him and drifted back to sleep, he knew that it was not the wind. He had heard it too. It was the same voice he had heard on previous nights, a low, despairing moan as of a woman slowly suffocating in an airless room, a woman gagged and confined. Had Francoise still been alive when Rousseau pushed her body into the chest? And what if she had been alive? Her body had been mutilated, the arms and legs missing when she had been found. Imagine that! He felt sick as he thought of the woman having to endure such pain. He tried to shut the image out but it hovered there, tormenting him.

He lay wide awake, feeling the rise and fall of Frances' breasts, and the cool air from the window, until, at last, he drifted back into a profound sleep.

CHAPTER THIRTEEN
HEAT

Denmark Street was a short street of Victorian artisans' villas lying at the rear of College Green. By the time Thomas had negotiated his way through the crowds of students and tourists in Park Street and cut down Unity Road, he was already sweating profusely. Removing his heavy jacket, he flung it over his shoulder, crossed the street into the shade on the opposite side and peered at the house numbers. He was looking for Number 13.

He soon found it. A red brick mansion with an incongruous bow window and worn window frames, it lay in the middle of the terrace and stood out in sharp contrast to its more prosperous looking neighbours. The basement flat where Andrew Holden lived was accessed by means of a dingy stone staircase, enclosed by rusting brown railings. Passers-by had thrown their litter down the stairs and there was an assortment of discarded newspapers and crushed cardboard boxes lying at the bottom, partly blocking the entrance to Flat 1B. Thomas descended the steps, kicking the festering rubbish to either side and found a battered front door, its glass pane replaced by a large section of plywood. He looked in vain for a bell, then rapped loudly on the door. The area smelled badly of discarded food and traffic fumes that drifted down from the street. He waited, but beyond the grimy window with its grey net curtain, nothing stirred.

He knocked again, this time louder. There was a sound of footsteps, followed by the sound of a chain being removed, then the door opened. A man with grizzled white hair and beard stood in the doorway. His high forehead was scarred above his left eyebrow and his vivid blue eyes peered at him questioningly. A thin roll-up hung from his bottom lip and his nicotine stained teeth were evidence of his heavy smoking. He was wearing tatty old shorts, a dirty brown T-shirt bearing the image of Che Guevara and from the lobe of one ear hung a silver CND pendant. His scrawny thin legs and worn leather sandals completed the picture for Thomas. An old hippy, Thomas thought to himself. From the inside of the flat a rank smell of cat urine and stale tobacco smoke drifted out to meet him.

"Andrew Holden?" asked Thomas, holding out his warrant card.

The man coughed, then removed the roll-up, a thin stream of tobacco smoke drifting from his mouth.

"Who wants to know?" he asked.

"DC Thomas. Avon and Somerset Police. I believe you knew Jack Slade? I'd like to ask you a few questions."

Holden coughed again, a deep, consumptive smoker's rattle which rippled through his body. Recovering his composure, he said:

"It's bloody inconvenient as a matter of fact. You'd best come in anyway."

Holden turned and shuffled down the dark corridor, scratching his beard, treading over a collection of discarded mail. Thomas followed him into a large sitting room with a high, ornate ceiling. Two battered 1950s-style sofas stood either side of a marble fireplace, which served as a storage place for piles of newspapers, faded paperbacks, pots and pans and a dented brass coal bucket. The mantelpiece above was strewn with unanswered bills and correspondence, old pipes, pipe cleaners, a large green ceramic tobacco jar and several tubes of oil paints. There was also a framed photograph showing a black-suited Holden, in his younger years. His dark hair and lean good looks bore little resemblance to the man who now stood in front of him. He was standing outside a church porch with one arm around a young woman with blonde hair wearing a Victorian-style wedding dress.

Holden went to one of the armchairs, and with both hands swept a pile of papers and folders onto the floor.

"Have a seat, why don't you?" he grunted. "Tea, coffee or something stronger? I'm having a scotch."

He moved to a scuffed oak sideboard and, pulling open one of the doors, took out a bottle of whisky, then slopped a large measure into a dirty glass.

"Water would do," observed Thomas.

Holden grimaced then disappeared into the kitchen. Thomas glanced round the room. It had the ambience of someone who had lived and worked in his own engrained squalor for years, a man who was preoccupied with a hard-living lifestyle to the detriment of his physical well-being. Holden returned, holding a mug.

"Here you are then. Now, what do you want to ask me?" he said, sitting down on a pile of sketch pads and rolling himself a fresh cigarette.

"Isabelle Le Conte and Jack Slade."

"What about them?"

"You knew both of them."

"I was Jack's best mate. Knew him for twenty years. We shared a number of gallery spaces together. And bars. One of the best painters I've ever known. He used to have the flat above mine. Originally he had this flat too. Used it as his studio space but when times were hard he rented it out to me."

"And Isabelle?"

Holden took a deep drag from his cigarette, then exhaled.

"Ah. Isabelle. What can I say? Beautiful, melancholy Isabelle. Yes, I knew Isabelle. I was in love with her, you know. Never told Jack. Hadn't the guts to. And it wasn't reciprocated. I loved her the first time I set eyes on her. She appeared at the Academy with her husband. Jack introduced me to her. I can't say I liked the look of her husband. Seemed a miserable bastard to me. Cold and controlling. She had those eyes – like a caged animal. I could tell there was something going on between her and Jack but the husband seemed oblivious to it. He was full of his own self-importance, stupid bastard. Typical academic. She often came to the flat – whenever she was over here from France. She'd turn up, spend the afternoon with Jack making love. I'd hear them through the floorboards. It was intolerable. Then, in the evening, she'd go back to her husband. God knows what excuse she'd given him. Last time I saw Isabelle was in '72. I've got a photo of us three somewhere here. Where is it?"

He stood up and began rummaging among the mess of papers on the mantelpiece.

"Yes, here it is. Here we are on the pier at Weston-super-Mare. Christ, I had black hair then!"

Thomas stared at the crumpled black and white photo. Holden was wearing a bowler hat with the words 'Kiss Me Quick' emblazoned across it. Slade, a short, powerful man with conventionally good looks, had his arm around the waist of a taller, elegant woman. She was wearing a tight fitting white T-shirt and a short pleated miniskirt which revealed long slender legs.

177

"When was this taken?" asked Thomas.

"Summer of '72. June I think. Yes, here it is, the date's on the back. She'd come over on her own. Said she'd left her husband and was going to shack up with Jack on a permanent basis. We'd gone to Weston because she was trying to contact a couple she knew. What was their name? The Stuarts? Yes – that was it. Owned one of those large guest houses near the front. Years back she'd had a child and they'd fostered it She'd lost contact with them for a while but she'd finally managed to track them down."

"And she visited them?"

"Yes. Jack and me found a pub on the front and spent the afternoon drinking. She met up with us a few hours later. She didn't say much apart from the fact that her daughter wasn't there, but I thought she looked upset. I didn't see much of her after that. Then, the strangest thing happened."

"What happened?"

"She disappeared. Into thin air. Slade had arranged to meet her at a pub in Whiteladies Road. She'd wanted to see a film. Some French film it was. Anyway, he waited for her at this pub near the Downs. I had a few jars with him in the saloon bar. But she never turned up. Strange thing was I'd seen her going into the cinema. I'd been walking down Whiteladies Road and was about to drop into the takeaway when I saw her going in. I thought she'd decided to give up on Slade, she was nowhere near the pub. Anyway, I waved to her but she didn't see me. That's the last I saw her."

"Isabelle was murdered not long after you saw her, we think. Her body was found recently in the grounds of a large house in Redland. You may have been one of the last people to see her alive."

* * *

When her husband had left, she took the small key from her purse and opened the door to her cupboard. On the table, nestling between the locks of hair and a large china doll, lay the sheet of paper she had photocopied the previous morning in Savageri's office. She switched on the small office lamp and, closing the door behind her, looked at each name and its accompanying photograph in turn. They were quite a mixture – quite a collection of nationalities. Some Asian names, some Italian, a few German names, but the great majority of them were French. She took a pen and began to make a series of crosses by those she was most attracted to. Beneath each image was the name and address of the student's host family along with their telephone numbers. Then she folded the sheet twice and slipped it into her pocket.

She picked up the china doll and began rocking it in her arms, staring down at its large blue eyes, tracing her finger along its cold porcelain cheeks. She had dressed it in a little crinoline skirt and matching blouse and its hair had been tied in ribbons. How cold and motionless it felt in her arms, not like a real flesh and blood child, a creature who would make demands of her, wake her in the night, bawl and defecate. By contrast, this small being was pliant to her will. She had no need to silence it, no need to strap the tape around its mouth, to suffocate its screams. Its coldness and stillness brought her temporary comfort. It helped assuage the terrible need that drove her to unspeakable acts.

Sometimes she would wake in the night thinking of those terrible deeds, unable to shut them out of her consciousness. She took the doll and placed it between the sheets of the pram then, extending the hood, began wheeling it towards the front door to the flat. She opened the door and began bumping it gently down the steps.

The road was deserted at this hour and a soft breeze helped lift the intolerable heat. She began pushing the pram down the long stretch of tree-lined road, pausing under a large tree to regain her breath. She was thinking of herself as a child, playing in the sand, the long expanse of beach stretching away to infinity. She could see her father reclining in a deckchair, a crumpled white hat on his head, his hairy chest scarcely concealed by a loud shirt. He had been wearing an old pair of khaki shorts and was lying back in the deck chair, *The Times* newspaper spread out over his bare knees and he had been smiling at her as she played. She smiled as she remembered him.

There next to him, was her mother, sitting bolt upright, her thin face twisted into a frown, her dark hair cut severely to her neck. She had that strange, otherworldly look about her. She was wearing a cheap printed dress, a prim velvet hat secured by a long hatpin and her black stockinged legs were trapped in an uncomfortable-looking pair of patent leather shoes. She had always looked as if she were securely pinned into place, never letting herself go, never exposing her emotions, encasing herself away from the world.

She had plastered her pale face with suntan lotion which made her look like a clown – it had made her want to laugh – but there was no humour in her, no fun. Every so often she would shout a command to the child playing in the sand, admonishing or cautioning her but the child resolutely ignored her. At last, she had left the deckchair and had begun slapping the child hard about the face and body until the child had cried. An elderly couple some twenty yards away sat staring and shaking their heads in disbelief but the woman simply ignored them.

The child had sobbed for a while, then sought the sanctuary of her father's embrace where she picked up the small china doll and began cradling it in her arms, trying to console herself. Her father had stroked her hair and had spoken to her softly. The woman had averted her gaze, then, taking a ball of wool from her bag, had begun to knit, clacking the needles with sharp, jabbing movements.

The child stared out to sea, watching the long roll of the waves, listening to the excited cries of other children, wishing she could be like them, wishing she were anywhere but here, oppressed by her tormenting mother.

The sea surged up the beach, driving long tongues of water into her moated sand castle, crumbling the sides of the towers. She was powerless to prevent its remorseless action. It was slow, measured and inevitable and cold as death.

The memory faded. She found herself standing at the edge of the park beneath a beech tree. By the small boating lake a child knelt with her mother, throwing pieces of bread on the water for the ducks. The mother smiled as she watched her daughter. She felt a pang of envy sweep through her. She wheeled the pram down the gravel path, crooning quietly to the doll, occasionally leaning over to adjust the sheets in the pram.

The sun was at its zenith now. She was sweating beneath the white mac and the dark wig was uncomfortable in the intense heat but she had no option but to wear them. She pushed the pram past the entrance to the park and crossed the main road by the crossing. A car slowed, its driver smiling at her. She smiled back and raised her hand in acknowledgement. For a moment she was someone else, and the terrible burden had lifted from her shoulders and her spirit lightened.

* * *

Ashley Geddings opened the door to Number 15 Thanet Road, then stepped inside and stood in the hallway, listening. The house was silent, only the traffic sounds from the street impinging on the quiet. Outside in the garden, scattered over the yellowing grass, lay a collection of abandoned toys and here in the hallway Michelle's blood still marked the yellow wallpaper. The house had a stale, fetid atmosphere.

He walked through into the living room and pushed open a window, allowing a gust of warm air to enter, then stared at the deep red stain on the carpet where Michelle had fallen. He caught sight of his own reflection in the mirror on the wall. The stubbled face stared back at him, his eyes red and sleepless. He sniffed his T-shirt. It stank of dried sweat. Walking upstairs and, stripping off, he turned on the shower, luxuriating in the scented bubbles of the shower gel, feeling the rivulets of water running through his hair. The smell reminded him of Michelle.

For two days Geddings had sat in the interview room as Glenister interrogated him. At first he had been 'helping the police with their enquiries' but during the afternoon of the first day the interviews had taken a very different turn. When Glenister had started probing Geddings about his relationship with Michelle Brown, he had begun to grow suspicious about the detective's motives. Glenister produced a bloodied T-shirt which Geddings had discarded when he had returned to his flat. Geddings explained that he and Michelle had been quarrelling over money and that Michelle had thrown a plate at him. It had hit him on the nose and he had bled profusely. Glenister sat listening, his lip curled in disbelief. Forensics would check the blood on the T-shirt, he said. He had no doubt that it would be Michelle's blood. And how did he account for the traces of blood on the soles of his trainers? He said he had gone back into the house and found Michelle in the living room. He knew he shouldn't have pushed past the policeman and entered the house but he had been beside himself with worry. He hadn't noticed that he'd been standing in the blood. He'd only realised when he'd got back to the flat. Then he'd changed his shoes. He'd told the other officer all this.

Geddings spent that night in the cell. In the morning he'd asked for a solicitor but Glenister wasn't having any of it. He was put into another room, smaller this time and there were just the two of them. He didn't like the feel of it at all. Glenister told him it would be better to make a clean breast of things now. It might get him a lighter sentence. He could say that he'd quarrelled with Michelle, then lost his temper and hit her. He'd panicked and hidden the murder weapon. His actions were understandable. It could be construed as manslaughter, not murder. Glenister gave him a pad and pen and told him he'd come back in half an hour. When he'd written the statement he'd allow him one phone call.

Geddings decided to sit it out. He wasn't going to be fitted up. When Glenister persisted and threatened to put him back into the cell, he retreated into silence. Glenister began to shout, then circled behind him in a menacing way but Geddings knew he just had to bide his time. Glenister had no real evidence. He knew the policeman was trying to build a case against him, but it was based on nothing more than assumptions. Geddings knew who'd killed Michelle and that man was Roy N'como. He tried to tell Glenister but he wasn't prepared to listen. Shortly after the police had visited 15 Thanet Road, Michelle had had a phone call. At first she had refused to tell Geddings who it was but when he pressed her, she had reluctantly told him that N'como had threatened her if she gave his name to the police. Michelle believed it was N'como who'd murdered Saunders and Aswere.

He'd had good reason to kill them. His son had been mown down by the car they'd been joyriding. He'd figured it out. It must have been them. One of his men had seen them careering down nearby Cambridge Terrace some fifteen minutes before the son had been seen bleeding in the road. They had often been seen in the area, sometimes toting guns from the darkened windows of their car, hurling abuse at passers-by, hurtling along the pavements scaring people half to death.

Although N'como could not find a witness to the incident itself he was sure they had killed his son, but despite his best efforts a wall of silence had faced him during his investigations. It had been Geddings who'd persuaded Michelle to give N'como's name to the police but now, with hindsight, he'd wished he'd kept his advice to himself. He'd known what N'como was capable of. It was unlikely that he'd murdered Michelle himself. He would have employed one of his men to do the job. But it was N'como who was responsible.

By midday Geddings still hadn't made a statement. Another detective with straight black hair had entered the interview room and whispered something in Glenister's ear. They left the room, then, five minutes later, Geddings had been released.

He walked to a coffee bar in Park Street and ordered a coffee and sandwich, then sat staring out through the window into the busy street. He knew what he had to do. He thought of Michelle's broken body lying on the carpet, the deep wound to the back of her head oozing blood, and the injustice of what N'como had done kindled a fire in his belly. She was his woman and he needed to sort it. He finished his coffee and sandwich, then caught a bus at the bottom of the hill.

When he finally got back to the flat, he took a shower, changed his clothes, then sat in the kitchen, drinking rum, figuring out what to do next. After half an hour had elapsed, he picked up the phone and rang the massage parlour in Waterloo Road.

* * *

"But the evidence simply isn't strong enough. It won't pass muster with the DPP," said Bottrell. They were sitting opposite each other in the interview room, The Formica desk was littered with empty coffee cups. Glenister looked weary, having spent the last two hours interrogating Stanton.

"What about the blood matches?" he asked.

"That's my point. There are none. Neither are there any fibre matches. We've examined all of Stanton's clothing, gone through it minutely. I'm telling you there are no matches."

"What about the footprint?"

"It's not even his size. And he doesn't own a pair of trainers. There isn't a shred of forensic evidence to connect him to the death of Rachael La Mer. All we have is a possible motive and a confession. And that was extracted by questionable means."

"What do you mean?"

"You know what I'm talking about. I saw you doing a number on Stanton."

"It got results, didn't it?"

Glenister was defensive. He knew his behaviour had been less than professional but he had been convinced Stanton was guilty.

"But it doesn't prove Stanton killed her. He was afraid of you. Afraid of having his private habits exposed."

There was a long silence. Glenister scratched his head.

"Alright," he said at last. "I'll tell you what we'll do. We'll release him, but we keep a tail on him. I remain convinced that he had motive. And maybe I was a little – heavy handed? We'll keep that to ourselves."

"Let's hope he does the same," remarked Bottrell. "He doesn't fit the profile. He's a voyeur. He's not a psychopath. He hasn't got the profile. Frances knows what she's talking about. She's good at her job. You should listen to her."

"Stuff the profile!" growled Glenister. "I go by instinct. Gut instinct. OK. We do it your way for now. But I hope to God you're right! It's been a useless day. Having to release Geddings and Stanton doesn't do much for our reputation."

"But you've done the right thing." said Bottrell quietly.

"Hmm." said Glenister, unconvinced. "Let's get the tail on the bastard."

CHAPTER FOURTEEN
ON THE DOWNS

At midday Thomas checked in to the office and was told the news about Stanton's release. It had been decided by Glenister that Evans and Bottrell would take it in turns to monitor Stanton's movements. When Stanton left, they took the car and followed him at a discreet distance as he made his way into Park Street, then caught the bus up to Redland. Thomas, who had informed Glenister briefly about his discussion with Holden, grabbed himself a sandwich from the snack bar on the corner of Park Street, then returned to the office to consult the telephone directory. There were six Stuarts living in Weston-super-Mare, but none of the first three he phoned were any good. On the fourth attempt he struck lucky. Alistair Stuart answered in a soft Edinburgh accent, his voice faltering with age. Yes, he would be in that afternoon if Thomas cared to visit him.

With the windows wound down, Thomas drove past Hotwells, out onto the A370, through the slumbering dormitory villages of Yaxley and Flax Bourton, past the great wood at Cleeve and down through Congresbury. Either side of the road, the Somerset hills slowly simmered in the hot summer heat. He drove on down onto the flat plains that lay to the east of Weston, tall hills rearing to his right against a cloudless sky.

He parked the car on the wide street that bordered the esplanade and made his way past the old pier where trippers jostled each other, some devouring bags of greasy chips, others strolling in family groups, eating ice creams that were already melting fast in the intense heat.

By the Victorian Winter Gardens he turned right and made his way through streets lined with august Edwardian villas, then climbed slowly upwards until he reached the imposing edifice of 25 Culloden Mansions, a huge four-storey homage to Edwardian grandiosity. Tudor chimneys, gothic windows and a round turreted roof completed the picture. Making his way down a flight of steep steps, Thomas found the intercom for Flat 3.

He pressed the button and there was a long pause, followed by the rattling of a door chain. A tall, cadaverous man of about seventy stood in the doorway. He was tidy in appearance, wearing a neat brown suit. His gold-rimmed half glasses gave him a somewhat owlish look.

"DC Thomas? I've been expecting you. Do come in. A cold drink perhaps? It's such a hot day."

Thomas stepped into the flat. The dark hallway opened into a large living room, stuffed to the hilt with bric-a-brac. Two green basket chairs stood either side of an ornate Victorian fireplace. The window at the far end of the room was concealed by a heavy velvet curtain in an effort to shut out the intense heat.

"Do you have any orange juice?" asked Thomas.

The smell of stale pipe smoke and cooking filled the room. Stuart shuffled into the kitchen, limping slightly, then returned carrying a tray with two glasses of orange juice.

"An arthritic hip I'm afraid," Stuart said, as if apologising for his disability. "I'm waiting to have an operation. Been waiting for the best part of a year now. Anyway, enough of my troubles, Detective Constable. What brings you here? You said on the phone you had some news of Isabelle."

Thomas told him about the discovery of her body. Stuart reached for his pipe and lit it.

"I'm shocked, I must say," he said. "Of course I hadn't heard from her for years. I knew she was living in France and that she was married, although not very happily, I'm sad to say."

"She wrote to you?"

"Yes. I kept all her letters. I am something of an obsessive collector."

"When did you last see her?"

"Oh let me see, the summer of 72, wasn't it? She dropped in to see me. She'd lost contact for a while. You knew, I take it, about her daughter?"

Thomas nodded.

"It was a pity she hadn't got my phone number. It was a wasted journey. She'd hoped to find Caroline, her daughter, but I had to disappoint her. You see, my wife and I were separated by then. She was a very difficult woman. Some would say she was disturbed. I believe that's the fashionable word for it nowadays. She was prone to acts of violence. Had a terrible temper. It was ten times worse when she drank. And she drank a lot. Wine and spirits. When her mood changed, she was like a demon. Nothing would stop her. I couldn't go on, it was destroying me. I sued for a divorce but the courts gave her custody and after that she moved to Redland. She refused me access. In fact I didn't even have her address. I only found out that she'd died when I read the article in the *Evening Post*. By that time Caroline must have been in her early-twenties. I did get a postcard telling me she was married and living in Redland. After that, nothing. Not even a Christmas card."

Thomas finished his orange juice.

"How did your wife die?" he asked.

"She'd been walking on the Downs, along by the cliff near the suspension bridge. It was a wet day and she must have slipped. Went straight over onto the road below. Didn't stand a chance. I organised the funeral of course but it was a small affair. Caroline turned up but she left as soon as the service was over. She hardly spoke, she blamed me for not intervening, you see. I should have done more to protect her when she was a child. But I was weak, that was the problem. I took the easy option, anything for a quiet life. I looked the other way. Much good it did me in the end."

"What was Caroline's married name?" Thomas asked.

"Campbell. Caroline Campbell. I'm afraid I don't have an address. Another orange juice?"

"No, I'm fine thanks. You say that your wife was prone to violence. Did Isabelle know she was like this?"

"She may have suspected it. She certainly knew about the drinking. I told her about that. She was concerned about Caroline. I tried to reassure her. I told her no harm would ever come to her while I was around. I'm not sure she believed me though. I have a hunch that's why she dropped in to see me that day. When she found out Caroline and her mother were no longer living here she became very upset. She accused me of lying to her. I felt so ashamed."

Stuart lowered his head, the weight of that remembered guilt weighing heavily on him.

"Do you have children?" he asked.

"No. I'm not married."

"Then don't. Life's a lot simpler without all that anguish. Who do you think might have killed Isabelle?"

"The answer to that is we don't know. It could have been someone who knew her well. We have interviewed a number of people who knew Isabelle during the summer of '72 when she disappeared. Is there anything you can think of that might be useful? Anything significant she might have said to you on that last visit? Anyone she mentioned who had threatened her?"

Stuart looked thoughtful.

"She did tell me she had received a letter from Hazel Slade."

"Saying what exactly?"

"Telling her to steer clear of her husband. You knew that they were having an affair?"

"Yes, Isabelle's husband told me about that."

"It was a marriage of convenience, nothing more. She was never really happy with him. Isabelle had a fiery temperament. Jean, on the other hand, was cold, detached, a cerebral creature. I only met him once and I can say I was not impressed. He had been married before, you know, to a French academic. They had a daughter called Anne Marie, a fine looking girl, very bright and very much her father's daughter. She became a teacher. She and Isabelle were quite close. She missed her mother. We shall all miss her."

The old man's eyes filled with tears.

Thomas left the flat, climbed the steps into the sundrenched street and made his way down Bury Hill. Far below him the sea glimmered in the blazing July heat like a great mirror and the sounds of the resort drifted up to meet him. Was it possible that Hazel Slade had killed Isabelle? Had she finally tired of Jack's peccadilloes, confronted his lover as she left the cinema on that July evening, then taken her revenge on Isabelle? It was not beyond the bounds of possibility. He made his way along the crowded front and found his car, baking in the afternoon heat. He opened the windows wide and sought consolation in an ice cream, then stood watching the slow roll of the waves as they snaked their way up the beach.

* * *

Roy N'como had just settled down in the office when the alarm bell in cubicle seven rang. It had been a difficult morning. He had arrived at 8am to find the front window staved in by passing vandals. Somehow they had managed to put a stick through the wire mesh with such force that the glass had given way under the pressure. Then, in the morning mail he had received final warnings from the electricity board and the rates department of the council. Coupled with this, the peptic ulcer which had dogged him for the past two years, seemed to have flared up again and he was conscious of a sharp pain in his stomach. Putting down a half-eaten roll he made his way down the corridor and opened the cubicle door. Jacqueline was sitting on the massage couch, naked. She was shivering uncontrollably and staring at him, her dark eyes filled with fear. She pointed to the door and opened her mouth to speak but before N'como could assess the situation, the door swung outwards, hitting him sideways. He keeled over, hitting his head on the edge of the massage table. In a moment an arm had forced his neck back and he found himself staring into Geddings face.

"How does it feel, Roy?" shouted Geddings, dragging him to his feet, twisting his arm behind his back so that he crashed face down on the table.

"Call the police, Jacqui. Quick!"

The girl fled from the room, Geddings ignoring her.

"This is for Michelle!" shouted Geddings, pulling the long-bladed knife from its sheath, then plunging it into N'como's back. He let out a low groan as Geddings pulled out the knife and raised it again.

"I want you to remember this. I want you to remember how it feels!"

But N'como was losing consciousness now, a thin trickle of blood oozing from his mouth. He tried to raise a hand to protect himself. His vision blurring, he slowly rolled from the couch and collapsed onto the floor, his eyes rolling, coughing blood.

* * *

Norman Stanton needed a drink. His nerves in tatters, he had returned to his flat just after midday. His persecution by the police was nothing new. When arrested in Weston-super-Mare, he had spent most of a day sitting in an airless interview room where he had been accused of being a sex pest and of interfering with one of his female students. It was an accusation which he found degrading. He was not a pervert. He might have strong sexual needs but a pervert he most certainly was not. He had a preference for young women. The police had made him out to be a paedophile. That was simply outrageous.

He removed his clothes and stepped into the shower, feeling the cold water running over his head and back. He rubbed the shower gel into his matted hair, then massaged his chest and legs vigorously. He would finish his shower, find some clean clothes, then walk up Whiteladies Road to the Six Bells. Then maybe a stroll over the Downs to regain his composure. Since he was no longer teaching he would have time on his hands.

He must have fallen asleep from exhaustion for when he looked at his watch it was much later. He found a thin linen suit, dressed, then made his way out onto the busy high street, the warm summer air smelling of petrol fumes and unwashed pavements. How dry and lifeless everywhere seemed now. He crossed the road, narrowly missing a car, and made his way into the snug bar of the Six Bells.

* * *

Despite having the windows wound down in Thomas's car, the air inside was sweltering. Bottrell had fixed a small, battery operated fan to the dashboard to alleviate the claustrophobic heat but it had made little difference.

"So Geddings has been arrested?" Thomas asked, sipping at his carton of orange juice.

"Late this morning. Glenister picked him up at his flat."

"And he admitted attacking N'como?"

"Made a full confession. Said he was proud of what he'd done. Told Glenister he'd done it for his girlfriend."

"What about N'como?"

"He's still alive – and conscious, though on the critical list. The first stab wound narrowly missed his heart. The second punctured his left lung. Glenister is at the Bristol Infirmary, hoping to get a confession out of N'como. He reckons if he can get him to admit to Michelle's murder, he'll probably cough for the other two."

"What about the forensic evidence?"

"He's got a search warrant for N'como's flat earlier this morning. Apparently the shoe print found at Thanet Road matches one of his trainers. There was also a pair of bloodstained trousers stuffed into his dustbin. It seems Geddings had it right."

"But why kill the girlfriend?"

"Because he was afraid of what she might know. Simple as that. She knew he'd killed Kevin Saunders and Michael Aswere. According to Geddings he'd boasted about it to one of the girls in the massage parlour. She turned out to be one of Michelle's friends. She had no real evidence of course, only hearsay. God, I hate jobs like this. What the hell are we doing here anyway?"

Thomas wiped his face with a crumpled handkerchief.

"Doing OBO on Stanton."

"A waste of time," Bottrell replied. "You know Glenister forced a confession out of him?"

"I heard that."

"Trouble is he has nothing on him. No real evidence."

"He had means and opportunity."

"Not nearly enough. And Glenister damn well knows it."

"So why did he release him?"

"I persuaded him. Told him the CPS wouldn't wear it."

"Listens to you, doesn't he?"

"He can be pig-headed at times but he usually sees sense in the end. How long has Stanton been in there now?"

Thomas glanced at his watch.

"At least an hour now."

"Look. I need a slash. Can you cover for me?"

* * *

Norman Stanton had been sitting in the snug for a good fifteen minutes before the students entered the saloon bar. There were six of them, three girls and three boys. At least two of the girls were under age but since Stanton had been suspended he wasn't in a position to make a song and dance about it. No, best stay where he was, out of sight. He sank down in the leather seat and cradled his beer glass. The tallest of the three girls went to the bar and began ordering drinks for the others. Some of the regulars turned to stare at her. Well they might, thought Stanton. He had noticed her on the first day of the summer term. She was a striking-looking girl and very mature for her age. Tall and blonde, she had a Scandinavian look with high cheekbones and a long, elegant neck. She perched herself at the bar and began chatting animatedly to one of the older boys as the bartender got her drinks. Stanton stared at the short miniskirt and her muscular thighs. He took a tissue from his pocket and dabbed at the sweat on his forehead as thoughts raced through his head.

Although he was at least some ten yards away from her, he was sure he could smell her perfume. Emilie. Yes, that was her name. He remembered it now. Emilie Gaboriau. She came from Brittany. She had sat in the back of his classroom and had been friendly with the boy Jean-Paul Le Pain. She was a beautiful girl and very mature for her age. He had intended to order a takeaway and return to the flat before watching some TV. There was a good film tonight. But no, he would stay here a little longer.

* * *

Bottrell opened the car door. Thomas was slumped over the steering wheel, snoring loudly. He shook him vigorously.

"Hey! Wake up!"

Thomas lurched, banging his head against the door frame.

"Christ. I'm sorry. I was out of it. Must be the heat. Drifted off."

Bottrell didn't reply. Instead he slammed the passenger door shut and, grim-faced, marched into the Six Bells. Within a minute he had exited again, shaking his head. He leaned in through the window, his face tight with anger.

"He's gone," he said. "He's given us the slip."

* * *

The Suspension Bridge was busy with afternoon traffic and strolling pedestrians. Stanton followed Emilie and Jean-Paul at a discreet distance, careful not to reveal his presence. On the other side of the bridge they paused to look down at the river. Stanton stopped at one of the viewing points, hidden from view by a group of German tourists, busy photographing each other. As they began to disperse, he saw that the couple had reached the end of the footbridge and had turned in the direction of Leigh Woods.

Under normal circumstances he would have called out to them, engaged in conversation, but now that he had been suspended from the school he felt uncomfortable and feared his behaviour would be considered inappropriate. No doubt the rumour had gone round. Norman Stanton was a sexual predator. After all, hadn't he been hauled off by the police for questioning? The thought of his pupils saying that made him boil with anger. He didn't know why he was following them now. He felt edgy and tense and old urges kept resurfacing. Something drove him. They wouldn't understand why he was following them. He just needed to see that young body and smooth flesh. That was all. Nothing else.

The couple had left the main road now and had entered the woods. He followed them down the narrow footpath, curious to know where they were heading. A long colonnade of beech trees rose on either side, shutting out the unremitting sun. Save for a tapestry of birdsong, the wood seemed empty at this hour. When he reached a footpath marker he stopped. The couple had disappeared momentarily.

He listened. He could hear the girl's voice some way off to his left. She was giggling and saying something in French. Following the direction of the voice, he pushed through a bank of dense ferns, then stopped and listened. The voice was closer now and was coming from the other side of a large beech tree. He made his way round the glade as quietly as he could. Finding refuge behind a small group of hawthorn trees, he peered out.

The girl was lying on a mossy bank, her legs raised. The youth was above her, kissing her passionately. His first instinct was to look away but he found himself staring rigidly at the tableau in front of him. He was fascinated by their lovemaking, the inexperience of youth, the fumblings, the lack of tenderness. He was saddened that the girl should offer herself so cheaply. He imagined himself in the callow youth's place, feeling the soft down on her slender neck, the rise and fall of her firm breasts, the dampness of her body... As his body responded to the lovemaking so he heard a sudden sound, some distance behind him, as of twigs snapping...

CHAPTER FIFTEEN
LEIGH WOODS

Ethel Miller took the lead from the tall hat stand and whistled. The small Jack Russell leapt from the sofa and appeared in the hallway, poised and shivering with anticipation.

"Come on, Johnny," she said, "heatwave or no. We'll go through the woods. It'll be cooler there."

Because of the intense heat of the day, Ethel had waited until early evening before leaving the house. Attaching the lead to Johnny's collar, she opened the front door and soon the little dog was bounding down the path, pulling his aged mistress at full stretch. Turning left at the end of the cul-de-sac, they made their way down a narrow footpath in the direction of Leigh Woods.

These walks were a daily ritual. Ever since her husband had died of cancer some six years ago, she and Johnny had taken this route through the woods. When Alfred had been alive it had been one of their favourite strolls. They had loved walking together as much as they had loved dancing together. Someone had once called them the perfect couple. But now Alfred was gone, it was just her and Johnny.

Even at this hour of the day the air seemed hot and humid. The little dog pulled ahead, barking joyfully. They were now on the outer perimeter of the wood where the vegetation was at its most green, despite the lack of rain.

"Hold on. Not too fast," urged Ethel. She undid the lead and let Johnny run. She was no longer as fit as she once was and these days her arthritic hip pained her. The dog ignored her, bounding ahead, a large wood pigeon starting from its cover. She looked ahead to see Johnny sitting bolt upright in the centre of the path, his ears cocked, growling.

"What is it boy? What is it?"

She glanced back down the path but there was no one. Then, through a gap in the trees she saw him, a young boy, sitting on a tree trunk. His arms were folded about his shoulders, his head was bent forwards and he was shaking. For a moment she felt afraid. Then, recovering her composure, she stepped forward, calling the dog to her.

"Are you OK?" she asked.

The youth looked up, tears streaming down his face. She noticed that his hands were bloodstained.

"Non... No. Please! Please help." He spoke with a strong French accent. Wiping away his tears, he stood up, his left hand supporting himself on the trunk of a tree.

"Please help!" he repeated. "An ambulance!"

"Are you hurt? What's happened to you?" she asked.

He turned and pointed to a gap in the trees.

"My girlfriend," he said. "You must help."

"Yes, yes, of course. Show me where she is."

The boy led the way past a tall beech tree. Ethel raised her hand to her mouth unable to believe the scene laid out before her. Spread-eagled on a mossy bank lay the body of a young girl. Her head was thrown back and her blonde hair spread out around her. She looked like some terrible, bloody Ophelia, the dark eyes wide and sightless, the mouth gaping and rimmed with dark blood. Across her slender neck a deep gash had been slashed, the edges of the flesh raised and livid. Her white T-shirt had been pushed up revealing the soft curve of her breasts and between them ran a crimson thread of congealed blood. The miniskirt had ridden up over her thighs. The effect was like that of some discarded shop dummy, cast aside on a rubbish tip, its legs and arms askew.

Ethel knelt down and examined the girl's face, feeling for a pulse in her neck.

"Who did this?" she asked.

She seized the barking Johnny and put his lead back on.

"Did you do this?" she asked, staring at his bloodstained hands.

"No, no!" he wailed, "We had said bad things to each other… how you say?"

"Do you mean you had a row?" asked Ethel helpfully.

"Yes. Yes. I went away. My head was full of the row. But I heard her screaming. I came back. I found her like this."

He covered his face in despair.

"Look. You stay here," she said. "I'll go back to my house. I'll phone for an ambulance. Wait here."

The boy nodded as Ethel made her way back down the path. She was shaking with shock but at the same time surprised at her own composure. That poor girl, she thought, so young, so beautiful. Transfixed by death like one of those delicate butterflies her father would net and chloroform. If Alfred had been here now, he would know what to do and say. No matter. She would have to make the best of it. She opened her front door, picked up the telephone and dialled 999. For a moment the awful picture of the dead girl's staring face drifted before her. Then she pulled herself together.

"Yes please. Ambulance and police. Someone has been murdered."

But all the while she was thinking to herself – why was she not wearing any knickers?

Reaching the top of Sion Hill, she paused and stared across, past the Greek columns of the old spa rooms, towards the great Egyptian pillars of the old Brunel Bridge. A long stream of traffic flowed across in the shimmering heat and far off, in the direction of Leigh Woods, she could make out the distant wail of a police siren. At times like this she missed the broad, open stretches of the beach and the cleansing power of the sea, the place where she had spent some of her childhood under the protection of a devoted father. Those were happier days before the dark cloud of her mother's alcoholism had taken its grip. This city was forever associated in her mind with that dark episode in her early life and it would never be properly eradicated.

She strolled to a bench and sat, facing the bridge, watching the little group of tourists and courting couples strolling across, sometimes stopping to peer over into the deep chasm below. From her bag she took a small, leather-bound volume bearing the title 'Les Fleurs Du Mal'. She traced the embossed cover with her forefinger, then slowly turned the pages, reading again the verses, awed by their profound melancholy. She treasured this volume. It had been a gift from Miss Thwaite, her English teacher. She had given it to her shortly before she left the school and over the years she had returned to it many times.

The poets taught that death was not something to be feared. On the contrary, it was a release from the suffering of the world, a journey into the great beyond. At the moment of death the soul gained its epiphany, a single moment when it took flight. The futility of life was then apparent. After all, wasn't life nothing more than a process of slow decay, from cradle to grave, a journey of toil and sorrow? Baudelaire had it right: we are all caught in a web of dissolution and decay and our only means of escape is through death. That was why she had chosen only those whose souls had shone like beacons to her. The eyes of her subjects were gateways to that other world.

She glanced up from the book. A small greenfinch had perched on the end of the bench, its black eyes watching her. She remembered the little yellow canary she had had as a child. Her father had bought it in a pet shop near Christmas Steps. She had immediately identified with the creature as it burst into spontaneous song in its cage. Each day when she drew back the curtains of her bedroom it would start its soliloquy. It became a source of endless joy, helping to lift the blackness of her moods. It was a creature of pure, unblemished spirit.

Then, one afternoon in late summer, she had returned home, having played tennis with a large, ungainly girl called Deirdre Fowler who, like her, was something of an outsider. They had become so engrossed in their match that they had hardly noticed an hour and a half had slipped by. As she had approached the house a terrible panic overcame her. She knew her mother's habits so well. By late afternoon she would begin her heavy drinking, a session which always continued into the evening. She would become maudlin and aggressive, seeking any opportunity to lash out at her daughter. Anything might motivate these attacks: a table not being laid correctly, a programme missed on the TV, a newspaper lying in the wrong place. But this evening it was the lateness of the hour. As she had entered the hall, she could hear the radio blaring out the six o'clock news. She had crept into the kitchen and found her mother standing by the cooker. She was as grim-faced as ever but, unusually, she did not raise her voice to berate her. Instead, she said quietly, "You'd best go upstairs and change."

When she had entered her room she saw what her mother had done. The bird cage was not in its usual place by the window but had been placed on the bed. Inside, on the floor of the cage, lay the canary. Its body was cold and stiff and its tiny head had been twisted and wrenched. Her mother had done this, just to spite her. It was her punishment. As she began to weep with sorrow and rage and was reaching in to the cold broken body, she heard her mother say, "That'll teach you to be late for dinner."

She had never forgotten the brutality of her mother's actions. Sometimes she believed that her mother was possessed. By what, she didn't know, since she had no faith in God or the Devil. The tortured, melancholy being who had plagued her father and driven him almost to madness would never alter. She knew that if she were to find release from this daily round of degradation, she would have to take drastic action.

Such an opportunity came in her late-teens. She was still living at home at the time, though, gratefully, she saw less of her mother now than ever before. She had managed to get a job in John Lewis's and worked long hours. In the evening she attended classes and so her presence in the flat was much reduced. However, Sundays were an exception. Although she got up late on purpose, her mother's drinking would often begin early and she would seek refuge in long walks on the Downs, not returning until late evening.

Then came the day she would never forget. She had set off shortly after breakfast, heading for Sion Hill. It was a wild, windy day and there were few people about at that hour. As she made her way to the Suspension Bridge, she happened to glance behind her. There was her mother, bent low under an umbrella. She was following her. How dare she? This was her world, not her mother's. The woman had become obsessed with her. There seemed to be no way of escaping her. She must have been curious to know what she did when she was out for so long. She was weaving drunkenly along the path and appeared to be talking to herself. As the drunken woman drew level with the camera obscura, she stopped suddenly and shouted to her daughter.

"Wait. What are you up to? Where do you think you're going? Come back to the house! Wait 'til I get you home!"

Her face was red with rage and drink and as her mother stood there swaying and shrieking, she finally knew what she must do to stop that foul tirade of abuse. Turning to face her, she shouted provocatively at her mother. She couldn't remember what she said, and her mother had responded with fury and strode towards her. They were level now, close by the footpath that ran level to the edge of the cliff. There was a point where the cliff had given way and part of the fence was down. She stood facing her mother, her back to the cliff, smiling insolently at her and calling her a drunken whore. Her mother lurched towards her and so she took her revenge. Stepping forward she raised her hand and struck her mother's face violently. The woman staggered back.

"I've put up with you for too long, you evil bitch! You've made my life a misery."

Her mother growled in anger and pain and lurched forward, raising her umbrella to strike but in a moment she stepped aside. Her mother staggered, desperately trying to regain her balance. One last shove sent her headlong over the edge of the cliff, her arms flailing, her body ricocheting off the rocks like a rag doll. For some moments she stood there transfixed, staring down at the crumpled body on the road below. A car stopped, its horn blaring loudly. Roused from her reverie, she glanced quickly about her but the footpath was quite deserted. Her heart pounding, she made her way along the path and did not stop until she had reached the other side of the Downs. For the first time she felt a deep sense of excitement. A laugh of joy bubbled up inside and burst out, like a great pressure valve being released. Her escape from this nightmare brought her an almost orgasmic feeling, something she had never felt so deeply before.

When she got back to the house she made herself a cup of tea, then sat in the living room, listening to the silence, knowing that never again would she hear the key in the door and feel that terrible sense of dread. She finished her tea, then went into the kitchen and began loading her mother's bottles into a large carrier bag. The smell of whisky and wine sickened her but her spirits were light now, lighter than they had been for a long while.

* * *

By nine that evening Leigh Woods was alive with police activity. The eastern perimeter had been closed to pedestrians and the murder scene marked off with the familiar barrier tape. Arc lamps illuminated the graceful beech trees which, in the gathering mist, stood tall and ghostly against the darkening sky. Glenister, looking pale, stood a few paces from the moss-covered tree trunk where the body had been found by Ethel Miller. Here, the white suited figure of Doug Walker crouched like some large preying mantis, accompanied by his female assistant, examining the victim's wounds with painstaking care and occasionally stopping to give instructions to his attentive companion. Glenister waited patiently, watching the moths careering into the bulbs of the arc lamps, clocking his fingers impatiently. At last Walker stood up, and, removing his surgical gloves, walked over to where Glenister was standing by the tree.

"Same MO as before," he said. "But our friend is growing careless. We have another footprint – quite a clear one, and it's the same small shoe size. We'll check it out but I swear it's identical with the one we found on Cabot Hill. Same murder weapon too. She was attacked while she was lying down. The attacker approached her from behind. You can tell by the direction of the blows. The first stab wound punctured her left lung, the second her jugular vein. She didn't stand a chance. You say there was a witness?"

Glenister pointed to the squad car beyond the barrier tape.

"He's in there. French student. Jean-Paul Le Pain. He was a friend of the girl. Says they had made love then had a row and he'd gone off to cool down when he'd heard her screaming. When he came back he caught a glimpse of someone making off in the direction of the road."

"Did he get a good look?"

"Not really. He thought it might have been a man but he couldn't really be sure. It was only a fleeting glimpse. He's suffering from shock. We'll try and get an artist's impression from him later when he's calmed down a bit, but I wouldn't hold out any hope."

"Did he touch the girl?"

"'Fraid so. Bloodstains on his shirt and trousers."

"We'll need his clothes. What about the old woman?"

"She's fine. Just her footprints, I guess."

"Oh, one other thing. There was a hair in the palm of the victim's left hand. She must have tried to defend herself."

* * *

Bottrell and Thomas arrived at 26, Cotham Lawn Road shortly after nine thirty. There was no reply on Stanton's intercom so Bottrell pressed the bell to Flat 2. An old woman wearing a hairnet and a dressing gown appeared at the door, looking distracted.

"Yes?" she asked with a frown.

"Police," said Bottrell, showing his card. "We want to speak to Norman Stanton. Is he in?"

"I wouldn't know. You'd best go up. It's the studio flat on the top floor."

They climbed two flights of stairs until they reached a small landing with a gothic window on one side and a door opposite marked Flat 3: N. Stanton. The door was slightly ajar and Bottrell pushed it open carefully and entered. The sitting room was immaculately tidy, books and magazines tidied into neat piles on the coffee table and there was a strong smell of beeswax polish. He went into the bedroom. The bed was made, a freshly laundered pair of silk pyjamas carefully folded on the salmon pink pillowcase. A small escritoire by the window lay open. On its gleaming surface lay a pile of papers and folders. Bottrell glanced at them. A will marked 'To Whom it may concern', several utility bills and an envelope marked: 'PLEASE READ – N.S'.

"John!" shouted Thomas, "you'd better come in here!"

Thomas was standing in the doorway to the adjoining room, his left hand gripping the brass doorknob.

"What's up?"

"Best look for yourself."

Bottrell walked past him into the room. In the centre stood an expensive looking massage table and on an adjoining table lay an assortment of bondage aids, including a hood fashioned

208

from PVC. The walls were lined with bookshelves, holding a vast array of erotic literature. But what caught Bottrell's attention was the figure at the far end of the room. Stanton's body hung by a rope attached to a hook in the ceiling. He was immaculately dressed in an expensive linen suit. His sober attire contrasted ironically with the bulging eyes and the black distended tongue which swelled from his open mouth. Thomas stepped forward and held the legs of the corpse as Bottrell retrieved the set of steps Stanton had kicked aside, then detached the rope from the hook.

"Best phone in," said Thomas laconically, walking towards the flat door.

Bottrell went back into the bedroom and opened the envelope. The message was written in a black, neat copperplate hand.

'Whoever reads this will find that I have left my affairs in order. My will and other principal documents are in a bundle along with my solicitor's name and address. I wish it to be noted that I hold the police solely responsible for the course of events which has led me to this ultimate decision, in particular Detective Inspector Glenister, who denied me my rights whilst in custody and who bullied me into signing a false confession to the murder of Rachael La Mer, for whose death I was in no way responsible. I feel that without a continued means of living and without the comfort offered by another human being, there is little point to my continued existence –

Norman Stanton.'

"What's that?" said Thomas.
"Suicide note."
He passed it to Thomas.

"Glenister isn't going to like this much," he said, after a pause.

"He can't say I didn't warn him. Stanton made a neat job of it anyway. Had the knot in exactly the right place. Even weighted his pockets down to make it easier. You spoke to Glenister?"

"He'll be here in about ten minutes with the pathologist. He's wrapping things up with the French boy at the moment. When he gets here I'll need to shift. Supposed to be interviewing a woman in Woodland Road about the Conte case. By the way, Glenister doesn't want the press poking about in this one."

"I can imagine."

CHAPTER SIXTEEN
CONCLUSION

Woodland Road was a long line of Victorian villas set either side of a tree-lined road. The terrace had seen better days, once offering a quiet, prosperous retreat to the wealthy classes of Bristol. These days the stucco had begun to crack, some of the front gardens were overgrown and the interiors of the great houses had been turned into bedsits and cheap guest houses.

Number 12 was no exception. Its worn front door still had an ornate door knocker but was scuffed by a succession of uncaring inmates. Fortunately for Thomas, Mrs Atherton, the landlady, had lived in the building for over two decades and knew the Campbell couple well.

"Come in dear, you look hot and bothered," she said, beckoning him into the dark hallway. Thomas stared momentarily at her worn face noting the ill-fitting wig perched on her head like some strange bird. He followed her into the large kitchen which had not altered since the 50s. Having been offered a glass of iced water, he perched uncomfortably on a stool.

"You said on the phone you knew Caroline and her husband quite well. Mrs Atherton."

"That I did. They lived in the top flat for about nine months, then bought a place of their own – somewhere in Redland I think."

"You don't recall their being visited by an older woman, I suppose? Dark haired, elegant looking. Spoke with a French accent?"

"I don't think so, no. I'm sure I would have remembered. Still got all my marbles, haven't I, Tommy?"

Reaching down, she patted a large white tom cat which was rubbing her legs vigorously. Thomas glanced at the rheumy-eyed cat and it meowed at him.

"He's friendly is Tommy. Stroke him. He won't bite."

"What were they like, the Campbells?" asked Thomas, as he bent to stroke the cat's head.

The old woman poured a large measure of gin into a glass.

"The husband was alright. A bit of a dear really. I got on well with him. Nice young chap, though a bit weedy. But she henpecked him something rotten. A nasty piece of work she was. Nice as pie at first, but then she'd turn. She was always shouting at him. She made so much noise Flat 4 complained to me about it. She used to have awful temper tantrums. Threw things at him. I don't know what her problem was and quite frankly I didn't want to know. In the end I told her they'd have to quieten down or go. It wasn't fair on the other residents. Screaming and shouting like a banshee. He worked but she never had a job. Just sat there in that flat, moping, or she'd be out at odd hours. He told me they'd lost a child – I suppose that may have had something to do with it."

"I don't suppose you've got a forwarding address for them?"

"I do as a matter of fact. I had a lot of mail for them after they left. Debts mainly from those shopping catalogues. I even had a debt collector turn up one day. In the end I got the address from the postman, I was so fed up with it. Don't suppose I should have done that but never mind. I'll go and get it for you. It's in my address book."

* * *

By late afternoon Anne Marie had returned to the flat in Pembroke Road. After seeing her father off at the airport she had sat in the bar for a long while, mulling over what he had told her. Since starting work at the university, she had phoned him in Paris on several occasions but without success. When finally she got through it was Anna the cleaning lady, who had told her that he'd left and was heading for Charles de Gaulle airport, already on his way to Bristol. When finally they'd met on the steps of the Wills Memorial building, he had broken the news about her stepmother. She had been distressed to hear what had befallen her, although she had barely known her. She remembered her as a tall, rather striking woman with dark hair and soulful eyes, who occasionally turned up at her father's apartment in Paris. It seemed that for most of her teenage years her parents had lived apart. Her father had talked to her about Isabelle with resignation in his voice, relieved to have found out the truth about her disappearance. Over coffee, Anne Marie did her best to console him before taking the taxi to the airport to bid him farewell. He seemed pale and gaunt and had lost some of his joie de vivre.

"Have the police a theory about who might have killed her?" she asked him.

"They don't really have a clue. The officer heading the investigation thought it might be someone who knew her quite well."

"The painter she was having an affair with – Slade?"

213

"No they don't think that's likely. Anyway, he died some years ago. I'm not sure we shall ever know now."

"Poor Isabelle."

She began rummaging about in the kitchen cupboard, looking for coffee beans, then found the packet, hidden behind a bag of sugar. It was empty. A thought occurred to her. The young woman in the flat downstairs might have some. When she'd first arrived she'd shown some kindness to her. Leaving her flat door ajar, she made her way downstairs.

* * *

"I know what the note says," said Glenister, snappily. "I'm more interested in the evidence."

He had his back to Bottrell and was examining documents in Stanton's writing desk.

"Ah here we are. Just as I thought." he said triumphantly, pulling two stapled sheets from the pile and waving them in Bottrell's face.

"What is it?"

"A list of students at the Belmont Language School, complete with photos and host addresses. And look, he's put a cross by some of the names, including Rachael La Mer and Emilie Gaboriau."

"It's circumstantial," Bottrell replied.

He was groaning inwardly. What did the French call it? An *idée fixe*, an uncontrollable obsession, that was it. No amount of persuasion was going to alter Glenister's opinion, he could see that.

"And we have the boy's testimony too," he continued, ignoring Bottrell's remark. "He's already told us he saw a man disappearing into the woods in the direction of the road."

"He says it might have been a man. He wasn't absolutely sure," Bottrell corrected him.

"Don't split hairs. It makes sense doesn't it? Stanton was released – much against my better judgement. Then he followed Amelie and her boyfriend into the wood, watched them perform. When the boy left after the row, he took his chance. If you'd kept a closer eye on him, she'd still be alive for Christ's sake."

"Thomas's fault not mine." Bottrell snapped back.

"Never mind that. It shouldn't have happened. I warned you about Stanton but you wouldn't listen. I should have trusted my instincts."

"But Frances—" he began.

"Never mind Frances—"

Just then Doug Walker appeared from the second bedroom.

"Sorry to interrupt the friendly chat, gents, but I thought you should know," he said, addressing Glenister, "I found a pair of shoes in the wardrobe with a quantity of mud on the soles, identical I should say to the soil type at the murder scene. I'll check it out at the lab."

Glenister smiled triumphantly at Bottrell.

"Is there anything else, gov?" he asked Glenister wearily.

"No, I think we're almost done here. I'll be making a statement to the press first thing in the morning. I'd like you and the team to be there. Where's Thomas, by the way?"

"Following up a lead in Redland."

"Alright, I'll contact him later. Make sure you let Frances know about the a.m. rendezvous."

"I will. Is that all?"

"Yes, that's it."

He glanced around at the contents of the room.

"Just look at this stuff. The sick bastard. I should have trusted my judgement. In future I will."

Bottrell didn't reply. Instead, he unzipped his white suit, folded it and walked resignedly into the hallway. What he needed was to get back to his flat, take a long shower and pour himself a large glass of whisky.

* * *

When she reached the downstairs flat, there was no one in. Caroline must have popped out for a moment, she thought. As she turned to go back to her flat she noticed the cupboard door in the hallway was shut but the key had been left in the lock. Naturally curious, she had often wondered what was in the cupboard when she had first moved into the flat. She turned the key and cautiously opened the door. It was dark inside but in the dim light from the hallway she could see the outline of a lamp on a low table. Stepping inside she fumbled for the light switch and the room was illuminated with a soft glow. She looked at the pine shelves. They were stuffed to the brim with antique dolls, shells and trinkets. She picked up a framed photograph from the table. It was a black and white shot showing a small child in a bathing suit clutching the hand of a tall, smiling man with dark hair. She thought the child bore a strong resemblance to her neighbour. This must be a picture from her childhood, she thought. She replaced the frame and began to examine the material on the shelves. It really was an odd assortment. One item in particular caught her eye. A book of poems, leather bound, with the title 'Les Fleurs Du Mal'. She was familiar with Baudelaire's verse. She opened the volume and began reading. It was a typical Baudelaire piece, full of images of death and decay. She had no idea Caroline spoke French. She had not mentioned it to her. Putting the book back, she moved on down the shelf. A large conch, several small shells and stones, a blackbird's wing and – what was this? A lock of dark hair, tied with a ribbon. Next to it, a black leather wallet. She opened it. There was a passport photograph of an elegant looking woman with black hair and opposite it a name: Isabelle Marie Le Conte.

A cold tremor passed through her. She found herself sitting down on the table, trying to calm herself. Isabelle Le Conte. Her stepmother. What was this doing here?

* * *

DC Thomas stared incredulously at the address on the piece of paper Mrs Atherton had handed him. It read: No 10, Pembroke Road. Wasn't that Bottrell's place?

"Excuse me but I have to go," he told the old woman. She looked disappointed.

"Sure you won't stay for some tea? I've got a home-made lemon drizzle. It's lovely to have the company you know."

"No, really. Thanks for your help, Mrs Atherton. I'll have to get a move on."

Leaving the flat, he walked out into the blinding daylight to the car, then picked up the radio receiver. A female voice answered. It was Frances. No. She hadn't seen Bottrell since early that morning. She thought Glenister had signed him off for the day. Glenister had wrapped up the case and wanted them all at the press conference scheduled for the following morning, nine sharp.

He drove right into Whiteladies Road, still thinking about the coincidence. He had hoped Bottrell might interview the daughter but he was probably off having a beer. No matter. He would do it himself. He turned into Pembroke Road and drove past the Language School until he found No 10. Parking the car, he crossed the road. A short flight of steps led up to the

217

imposing front door of the building and the front door lay ajar. There, on the nameplate were the names Caroline and Jack Campbell.

* * *

Bottrell got back to the flat early in the afternoon. Flinging his jacket onto the sofa, he stripped off and stepped into the shower. The cold water sluiced over his head and shoulders and he stood there for a good five minutes, washing the sweat and grime from his body, glad that at last events were moving towards a conclusion. Not that he agreed with Glenister over the business of Norman Stanton. He had been precipitate and bullish about the affair, too eager to get a result. What if Frances was right and the killer was still out on the Downs? It was a gamble on Glenister's part and one which lacked proper forensic evidence. Stanton's confession counted for nothing. He may well have had designs on some of his female students but that didn't make him a killer. Glenister's dislike of Stanton had surely coloured his judgement? He turned off the shower and, wrapping a towel round him, walked through to the kitchen and poured himself a large whisky.

At the window he paused and looked down. The road sweltered in the afternoon heat and a cloud of dust rose from the melting tarmac. How could it be this hot? It had to be in the 90s. He was about to turn away when he noticed a figure making her way to the front door. She was wearing a dark blue coat and a short skirt and large black sunglasses obscured the upper part of her face. God she must have been sweltering, he thought. There was something odd about her appearance. What was it? The hair. Yes, that was it. Surely it was a wig. It was cut short to the neck, giving her a somewhat mannish look. She stopped at the front door, peered up and down the road, then walked into the house. Who was she? She seemed to be familiar with the place and something about her appearance nagged at him. What was it?

Reaching for the glass he walked into the bedroom, dressed, then poured himself another drink. He looked at his watch. Glenister was probably even now celebrating with Evans in the nearest pub and here he was, drinking alone. He needed some air. Pulling himself together, he finally left the flat, feeling refreshed and invigorated.

On the landing he paused, noticing Anne Marie's flat door was wide open. He could hear music playing from somewhere inside. He knocked but there was no reply. He could smell cooking. He called out but there was no response. He hoped nothing had happened to her. Walking in, he looked around but there was no sign of her. Feeling a vague sense of alarm, he made his way down the stairs.

*　*　*

For some hours after killing Emilie Gaboriau she had wandered along woodland paths, deep into the woods. The great trees on either side of the path reared like silent sentinels and the air was full of bird song. Here among the trees she felt safe. Her spirit was lifted by this wild, deserted landscape. There was nothing here which acted as a landmark for the man-made world which she had grown to hate. She had not felt like this since she had been a child, playing on the beach, the sound of the waves lulling her, a reminder of the great primal source of being.

She had reached the eastern perimeter of the wood. Here she was able to look down over the limestone cliff. In the distance she could see the derricks of the docks, while far off the city centre shimmered in the heat. She could smell the river from

219

up here, taste its tangy earthiness. If she had more courage she would have hurled herself into the abyss below, plunged herself into the cold water, surrendering her soul to oblivion as the poets had written.

Moving closer to the edge of the cliff she removed her bloodstained coat and threw it over. She watched as it drifted down through the air like a great swan until it became entangled in a bush halfway down and flapped helplessly in the slight breeze. They'd never find that she thought.

She would catch a bus into the city centre and buy some new clothes, then return to the flat. Jack would not be back from his insurance conference until the next day, so there was no rush. She would shower, make herself a meal and relax. She would be careful to avoid returning through the wood in case the police were there. She only hoped the boy hadn't seen her. It had been a gamble, one that had nearly backfired. Walking north she made her way back to the main road.

Once in the city a terrible fatigue began to oppress her. Moving in and out of the crowds, she was jostled this way and that, hating the proximity of others, until at last she reached the air-conditioned interior of a large department store. Here she purchased a dark blue coat and skirt. Slipping into the public toilets she changed, then made the slow ascent up Whiteladies Road. She felt numb now, detached from reality. This terrible fatigue had invaded her, leeched her strength. She kept seeing the body of the young woman, her pale flesh against the green of the moss. Her sightless eyes stared back at her, her mouth a well of crimson blood. Much as she tried to obliterate that terrible image from her mind, it haunted her.

Dodging the traffic, she turned into Pembroke Road. Her legs were leaden, her mouth dry. She must be dehydrated. She felt a desperate urge to get back to the sanctity of her room and collection. Reaching number 10, she opened the gate and stopped, making sure the coast was clear. She should have got rid of the wig and glasses, or at least made an effort to conceal them before she returned to the house. Normally she would have done this without thinking. She couldn't afford to be seen in them so close to home. Usually she was clear-headed and very focused but now she felt fazed, detached. Was she losing her grip? She would conceal the wig and glasses in her special place. Perhaps she would need them again? Rational thought was slipping away now. After the last murder something had happened to her. She had begun to sicken at the thought of her actions.

Inside the house, the air was cool and refreshing. There was a faint smell of lavender and the sound of music drifting down the stairwell, probably coming from one of the top flats. She got out her key and had opened her flat door when, glancing back down the hall, she noticed the door to her cupboard was slightly open. She froze for a moment. She had remembered locking it when she left, but she must have left the key in the lock. Stupid, stupid thing to do. She was always so careful. What if someone had opened the door and poked around in her precious belongings? The thought filled her with dread, then anger. She stood in the hallway, listening. There were sounds coming from inside. She peered through the crack. A young woman. She was looking at something, a wallet, and she was weeping. It was Anne Marie. That must be her music she could hear. No one else would be in at this hour.

A terrible anger took hold of her. She entered the cupboard and shouted at the intruder. Seizing her by the hair she brutally pulled the girl up from the table and slammed her into the wall. Shouting uncontrollably she yanked the terrified girl across the hallway and pushed her roughly into the flat. The girl was holding the wallet, pleading with her, but she heard none of it. She slammed the door then pushed Anne Marie down, banging her head onto the table. The girl lay there moaning, stunned by the impact. Taking the knife from her pocket she grabbed the girl's hair again, cursing her, and cut off a large chunk of it. The girl pushed at her with her free hand. She was shouting back at her now, her eyes wide with fear.

Still she did not hear the words. The red mist had enveloped her totally. The girl was saying something about a stepmother but none of it made any sense. She raised her knife, aiming at the girl's chest but as she lunged the girl raised her hands and the blade ripped across her wrist. She swore at her, then grabbed her by the throat. She had her now. She was pinioned on the table, pleading with her. She brought the knife to her throat, then pressed, cutting her.

"I'll teach you!" she whispered, barely able to control her fury. "This is just a taste of what's to come!"

There was a sound from behind her. Whirling around she saw a man standing in the doorway of the flat, staring in, astonished at the scene unfolding before him. He must have broken in, she thought irrationally. How dare he? Behind him stood another, taller man. She recognised him. He was from the top flat. As they moved into the room, slowly approaching her, she released the girl, then lashed out with the knife, shrieking insanely. She slashed the tall man's arm, growling like a beast, but he grabbed her by the wrist. She was yelling at him, punching him wildly but the other one had her by the hair now and his knee was on her chest. Then a hand closed over her mouth and something cold and hard clicked round her wrists.

Afterwards, she remembered little. She recalled sitting in the kitchen, her mind full of disordered memories and fractured images. One of the men had wrapped a bandage round his hand where she had cut him. The other man was comforting Anne Marie and tending to her injuries.

* * *

"OK. I'll admit it. I was wrong about Stanton," said Glenister, reluctantly. "But the circumstantial evidence was convincing."

Bottrell was by the open window, back at headquarters. Outside, dark clouds were gathering over Brandon Hill. In the distance there was a roll of thunder.

"Anyway," Glenister continued, eager to change the subject and directing his gaze to Frances Leadbetter, "how's the French girl doing?"

"Recovering well," said Frances. "There's some wounding to her face, hands and throat. Some concussion too. Caroline was really very brutal. She'll need time to get over the shock, of course."

"She had a lucky escape," agreed Bottrell. "It was pure chance I was back at the flat and that I heard her. Five minutes later and we would have been too late. I was glad of the backup."

Bottrell smiled at Thomas.

"You interviewed the husband yet?" Glenister asked Thomas.

He nodded.

"He told me he had no idea about the cupboard in the hall. Says his wife told him the key had been lost, so he never bothered trying to open it. She must have been very careful when she used the room. Personally I'm inclined to believe him. He's a strange bloke and not over-bright. It's almost as if he didn't know his wife. Seems he was completely dominated by her. He told me she used to fly into rages and threw things at him. It took him a while to admit it mind. Thought it was a reflection on his masculinity, I suppose. His right arm was badly scarred where she'd taken a knife to him some months back."

"I know the feeling," Bottrell commented ruefully.

"And he didn't think to report the attack?" enquired Glenister.

Thomas shook his head.

"No. He kept quiet about it. He must have been terrified of her when those moods came on her. He almost broke down when he began to open up."

"Being an abused husband is a difficult thing for a man to admit," Bottrell said.

"And he knew nothing of the French connection?" asked Evans.

"Nothing. Though neither did Caroline Campbell of course. The adoptive parents never told her. Hardly surprising since the adoption was illegal. She was barely six months old when they took her back to England, although they did visit France on a subsequent occasion. How did she take it when you told her she'd killed her own mother?"

"Difficult to say," said Glenister. "She hasn't confessed yet to any of the murders. The evidence is overwhelming, however. Her cupboard is being searched thoroughly. Walker will be examining the knife and her clothes, and shoes of course. She had a list of the language school students with their addresses. Turns out she was a cleaner at the place and was able to take the list from Savageri's office. She'd even highlighted the names of her intended victims.

"I showed her the photos of Emilie Gaboriau. Set them out on the table to gauge her reaction. At first she said nothing. Then she pushed them aside and began ranting on about her mother.

She meant her stepmother of course. She was red with anger, shouted about this woman who'd abused her, tormented her, locked her in a cupboard when she was a child. She was in a frenzy. Bottrell and I tried to restrain her but she had the strength of two men. Banged her head against the door, screamed abuse at us. It took us a while to get the cuffs back on her. Eventually she calmed down. When I told her about Isabelle Le Conte being her natural mother she fell silent."

"She's deeply traumatised," observed Frances. "And still full of anger for her tormentor. But that's not surprising. Based on what you've told me about her background, there's a pretty clear picture of sustained abuse emerging, probably going back to her childhood. In a sense it wasn't Anne Marie she saw in that cupboard – it was her adoptive mother. Same for the other victims too. For years she's been obsessed by the need to kill over and over again. She'll never exorcise that ghost. That cupboard represented for her a final refuge, a place where she could collect small trophies, bits and pieces of her tragic past, try to make sense of things. A lock of hair, the odd belonging, her doll collection. I suppose the dolls would have been her family – easy to control, silent and totally emotionless, her comfort blanket."

"And what about the duct tape?" Glenister asked. "What did that signify?"

"The mouth was symbolic of her stepmother's scorn and abuse. By taping up her victim's mouths she could try to silence the ogre from her past. But never completely, it seems. God knows how she must have suffered. Cruelty begets cruelty. Didn't someone say that once?"

* * *

225

By five o'clock the meeting had ended and the team had adjourned to the pub. Only Bottrell and Frances remained. They stood by the open window, holding hands, watching a succession of dark clouds gather over Cabot Tower. The fierce sunlight had now gone and the air was close and humid. As they stared out over the city a fresh breeze fanned their faces. Then came a sound they had not heard for such a long time. The sound of rain. Quiet droplets, slow at first, splashing their faces, cooling their skin. And soon a deluge. Great sheets of rain, cascading over the rooftops, choking the gutters, while in the distance forked lightning lit the blackened sky. They leaned out of the window, laughing together, drinking in the wet, welcome air as the rain cleansed and purified the soiled, grimed city.

Bottrell turned and kissed Frances and they turned and walked back across the room, down the stairs, into the glistening streets of the city where drenched city workers were standing, smiling and laughing as the welcome rain washed away the grit and dirt.

EPILOGUE

White.

White and cold. Overhead, bright fluorescent lights. Bruised head aching. Memories of soft sand, waves, salt water on lips. Gulls screeching.

A dark cupboard, filled with shells, dolls, a broken bird's wing, safety.

Light falling on polished wood.

Light breaking through trees.

A child playing in the sand, laughing.

"Carrie! Carrie!"

"Who's calling me?"

"Where are you?"

"I'm here, mummy. I'm here."

That face. That one face. Dark hair. High cheekbones. The mother. Her own mother. Her own flesh and blood. The smell of spilt blood. Hands wet with blood. Eyes staring, mouth bloody. So much blood. So much...

She opened her mouth. Like a great wave, the scream welled up and burst into the silence of the cell.